BENEDICTION FOR A THIEF

THE ATHERTON TOWN ESCAPADES

A Novella

L. A Sykes

Close To The Bone Publishing

Close To The Bone
an imprint of Gritfiction Ltd
Northampton
Northamptonshire
NN4
www.close2thebone.co.uk

First published in Great Britain in 2025 by Close To The Bone

Copyright © 2025 L.A. Sykes

L. A. Sykes asserts the moral right to be identified as the author of this work in accordance with the Copyright, Designs and Patents Act 1988

ISBN 979-8-61586-965-5

All rights reserved. No part of the book may be reproduced, stored in a retrieval system, or transmitted in any form or by any means, electronic, mechanical, photocopying, recording or otherwise, without the prior permission of the publisher.

The characters and events in this book are fictitious. Any similarity to real persons, living or dead, is coincidental and not intended by the author.

First Printing, 2025

For Sienna and Harry

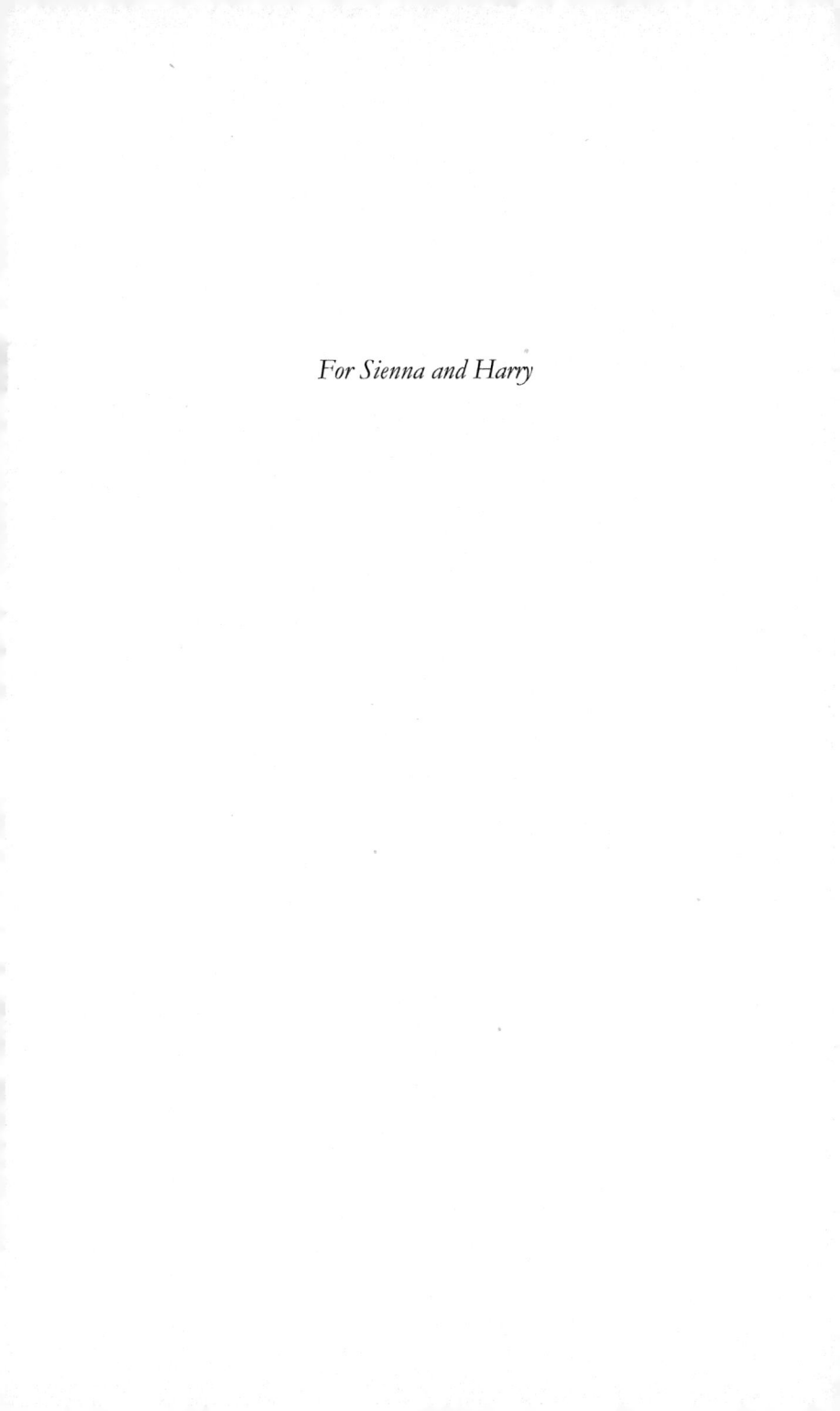

"Anger is an energy"

John Lydon

Prologue

I crave for sleep yet hate to dream.

Dead and the living come to whisper in this old town.

Take comfort from history, for those who strode the fields of Agincourt and mounted up against the Jacobite Rising made homestead in this Bronze Age settlement, this ancient Roman road between Coccium and Mamucium.

Traverse time to when the coal pits mined and the cotton spun and weaved. Workers churned out nails and scythes and nuts and bolts as the wind harried smoke plumes, flowing with the seven brooks.

Watch local Luddites hanged in 1812 for trying to defend what are now the derelict shells of discarded industries; mills whose towers taunt the sky.

An urban sprawl and endless dense rows of red brick terraces and cobbled lanes stretch to the centre, Market Street, with its sandstone obelisk and St John the Baptist's turrets at the top of the narrow walkway of late Victorian shopfronts now gaudy.

The town, encompassing Hag Fold, Hindsford and Howe Bridge, whose name derives from Old English, thrives on.

I walk the tarmacked roads and concrete paved hills to the dirge of traffic and bask in the surviving snatches of grassland and ponder what life was like for folks in bygone eras; listen to what they whisper about the way we live our lives today.

Especially after the summer I had.

A summer of being the hunter and the hunted

A summer of drugs and guns

A summer of laughter and lamenting

A summer I'll never forget

1

I was the first, and likely last, private investigator to set up business in Atherton Town and it was on my first official job that I kissed goodbye to whatever slither of spiritual salvation I had left, on a fine early June Wednesday morning, when I planted a bug in the confessional booth of Saint Richard's Church on Mayfield Street.

I had debated the ecclesiastical unethicality of my doings in taking such a step but concluded that the saving of petrol from not having to tail my target by vehicle in times of both austerity and the dawning impact of pollution to God's Earth more than likely outweighed electronic eavesdropping from within the sacred space.

I was also acutely aware that Father Percival Kay wouldn't take my money to provide the contents of the confession of my target. It wasn't that the priest was not corruptible; it was down to the fact that the priest still despised me as the prime suspect in the theft of the giant crucifix in 1991 and had never contemplated forgiveness for such sacrilege.

I tentatively stepped under the arch of the beautiful church and took in the pale blue alcove, dipped my finger in the font and made the Sign of the Cross for the first time in over twenty years. Made my way into the confessional booth and knelt down.

Cleared my throat, put on my best Johnny Cash baritone and said, "I shot a man in Reno just to watch him die."

Couldn't resist it.

Father Kay let out a low whistle from the other side of the thick red curtain. "Don't take the piss. Have you finally come to confess your thefts, Jacob Gibfield? Your soul needs redemption."

I clipped the bug under the ledge of the partition. "How did you know it was me? Isn't this supposed to be anonymous?"

"Get fucking real."

"For the record I never stole the crucifix. And it was twenty seven years ago. I think it's about time you got over it and offered compassion for the thief."

Father Kay ripped back the curtain and reached for my neck but I scrambled out of the booth and jogged to the door.

"I'll tan your blasphemous arse for you," bellowed at my back all the way outside.

I nipped to Bar-Be-Chic for a Dawson's Pie and reversed the beat-up white transit van onto the cobbles of Cambridge Street around the corner from Saint Richard's. Munching on my grub, I clipped in my earphones and got comfortable in the back to wait for my target.

***

One Mrs Ricketts was my first client in my new, official career as PI. She'd walked in my office above the barber shop opposite the post office on Market Street on my first day on the job two days earlier. She was mid-thirties, prim and dressed in a tight-fitting powder blue pantsuit with low heels. She was all business and pretty enough to remind me of the loneliness I harboured since my fiancée left me after my disgraceful sacking from the psychiatric hospital.

"Mr Gibfield, it's my husband, he keeps crying in his sleep. At first I thought he was, you know, cracking up under the stress of his job, especially since he's devout."

"What does he do?"

"He's a tax collector."

I struggled to keep a straight face.

Mrs Ricketts gave me a stern look. "He used to work at the disability centre until the council closed it down and he couldn't find anything else."

"Sorry."

I'd read stacks of PI novels and figured now was the time to put on my compassionate, empathetic air so I might get laid. Tried, "I can see the clash in morality can cause such spiritual dissonance. I struggle with it myself in my profession."

She gave me a perplexed glance. "Why? How long have you been doing this?"

"Couple of days, officially. Don't worry, I've got all the manuals and I know this business inside out." Which meant I'd read the aforementioned novels to pass time on the night shift at the psychiatric hospital. That was before being sacked for stealing thousands of boxes of neuroleptics and benzos to sell, with my mate Ronnie Finkell acting as my link to the street.

She hesitated, looked me up and down in my one and only suit (cream coloured) and lilac shirt with an air of mild disdain and apprehension. I could kind of tell she was thinking that at least my fees were relatively cheap.

"The longer it's gone on, the more I think it's another woman."

"What makes you think that?

She blushed. "Wet pyjamas."

"He pisses the bed?"

"Of course not. I mean, well, you know."

"Oh, wet dreams. Got you." I looked her up and down and went with, "If I was sleeping next to you I'd be having wet drea-"

She cut me off by looking me up and down again and raising her eyebrows. "Here's a copy of his passport photo and his route to and from work. I assume you'll be tailing him. I want A3-size pictures if possible."

I made a mental note to burn the suit and nodded along. "Anglican?"

"Catholic. St. Richard's."

"Call me Wednesday evening." Confession day. I reached to shake hands but she recoiled and darted down the stairs, gaining a couple of wolf whistles from the lads waiting for a haircut.

The elderly barber, Victor Barnes, said in his strong Caribbean lilt, "Leave the lady alone people. She be free to walk where she wants without you hooting at her. How goes it, Jacob? Business booming already?" He gave me a smile and I winked and returned it, feeling pretty good that I was up and running.

The laid-back afternoon ambience was broken as a ragged Fiesta with no license plates screeched up and mounted the kerb. Three geezers with their faces hidden by balaclavas sat inside. The passenger door swung open and a house brick flew through the air, shattering Barnes' window. The assailants screeched off beeping the horn.

A note had been attached to the brick with an elastic band. Victor picked it up from the midst of glass shards mingling with hair. Read: *Live in Fear.*

He handed it to me and said, "You've been above my shop for two days and they want you out already."

I laughed despite myself. "Don't worry. I'll find out who those fuckers are."

"I ain't worried, not in this Town."

"You let me off a month's rent and I'll get those shitbags to fix your window. How's that?"

"How you goin' to find 'em?"

"Trust me, I'm a gumshoe. It's my job. You calling the cops?"

Victor laughed out loud, surveyed the damage again and shook his head. The customers were already sweeping up for the old man.

"PC Chase is an old friend of mine. Want me to do the honours?"

"Too much fuss. Educate don't retaliate is what I say. Plus, I'm insured." He gave a weary grin.

I shrugged and admired the old man's grit. I seemed more shaken up by it than he was.

I'd planned to be able to one-man-band it until business picked up but already had a feeling I might need more than the back up of using Fez's name. I shuddered at the thought I'd actually need the man in person. First up though were my priorities of collecting a confession for Mrs Ricketts and sorting out my camp bed in the back room of the office.

***

Here now on the Wednesday I finished my meat and potato pie and threw the foil out of the window as a jerky, nervous looking fellow in a brown baggy suit that matched Mr P. Ricketts' passport photo scuttled into the church. I hit record and listened:

Mr P. Ricketts: Forgive me father for I have sinned…I feel so ashamed. I've broken my marriage vows and fornicated with another woman, Father.

Father Kay: Put a donk on it and shave your pubes off so you don't catch crabs. Next.

Mr P. Ricketts: You what?

Father Kay: It's the Third Millennium; no one gives a fuck anymore. Next.

Chuckling to myself in the back of my van, I watched thirty seconds later as the tax collector stumbled out looking bewildered. Job done.

Out of curiosity I listened to the next confession. A crackly voice said, "Father, I'm hearing God's voice. What shall I do?"

"Pack your shit and go straight to the nuthouse. I'm a priest not a shrink for fuck's sake."

I burst into hysterics, wiped the tears out of my eyes and disconnected the bug. Put the van in gear and drove down past the park to the bottom of Hamilton Street, turning right onto Leigh Road, where the proud Cenotaph stood; our town's memorial where the wreaths were laid every November for the giants on whose shoulders the country stood to this day.

As I turned into Leigh Road I rapidly hit the brakes and skidded to a halt.

Out of the bushes near the park gate a barefooted man, with what appeared to be a dead cat for a belt, sprinted into the road. He was wiry and lean and his mandible swung askew and he looked suspiciously like my man-in-the-know, Ronnie Finkell.

The van stopped inches away from the figure, who looked up briefly, wild-eyed with dark hair stuck up and littered with bits of shrubbery. He looked left and right and then darted back over the wall and into the very same bushes. Following him came PC Colin Chase, equally wild-eyed, blowing hard and pumping sweat in full uniform. He caught his breath, rubbed his hand over his now hatless head, saw me stationary in the middle of the road and ran over motioning to wind down the window as a line of cars backed up behind me.

"Alright mate, what's going on?"
"Your pal, Finkell. I'll kill him." Colin said.
"What's he done this time?"
"I'll tell you later. Where are you living?"

"Old Victor Barnes' barber shop. Kipping in my office upstairs till I get a wedge."

"Office?"

"Aye, I'm a private investigator."

PC Chase looked bemused for a second until his face creased and let out a snigger.

"I'm serious. Come round tonight for a drink. Best get moving."

A plethora of honking horns and abuse sounded up Leigh Road until I shunted the van into gear and sped off up Mealhouse Lane. Parked across from the public toilets near the sunbed shop and walked to the office past Victor's boarded up window which reminded me that I had a free month's rent to earn. And one of the men I needed for that was the apparently feral Ronnie Finkell.

2

It was a favour done for an old friend that started it all. I was working the nightshift at the psychiatric hospital back then, and one night in April a lady was brought in by a different old friend, the aforementioned PC Colin Chase. He'd found her on the bypass linking Atherton to Leigh, stood on the edge of the road, waiting for a lorry or coach to dive under. He detained her under Section 136 and brought her to the hospital where I was sat reading after the night medication round had just finished because most of the patients had gone to bed and it was relatively quiet.

While we waited for the on-call doctor to come and do the assessment I tried to get her to open up and talk a bit but her face was swollen and she wasn't having any of it other than name and abode. I left a female colleague to sit with her and re-checked her notes. I recognised the address and said to PC Chase, "You know who this is, don't you?"

"Should I?"

"Your old partner's cousin."

DS Mark Reed was Colin's old beat walker buddy before he'd got the promotion. We'd all known each other from childhood; played football together right through to our late teens until the dream of being a pro hit the reality of keeping a roof over our heads. Some of the lads went to C of E schools and some of us went to the Catholic schools and we'd never even heard of sectarianism. Eventually we'd all drifted off; me into the NHS in the psychiatric hospital, Colin and Mark to the police, Simon 'Hairband' Braggins on to the doors, Chris 'Fez' Ferry to the army and Ronnie 'Hag Fold Hurricane' Finkell first into boxing then down into the drug world.

"Shit. I think you should ring him."

"He was your partner. You fallen out?"

"He's been assigned to the drug squad."

I let out a chuckle. Colin was the biggest coke head out of all of us. I didn't really bother except the odd dabble on a Saturday night. Although I did have the minor side-line in stealing thousands of tablets to sell on the street. Finkell was a speed freak extraordinaire, knew everybody, and like I said, was my distributor alongside his own doings to fund his habit. If Mark was on his game we'd all be fucked and Colin saw the funny side too.

"Do we need to be worried?"

Colin's smile faded a little. "We'll have to watch him. He's got serious ambitions about making it to the top, and he's into all this healthy clean living stuff now. Worse than Fez."

Fez had the army fitness and strength drilled into his fibre, despised all drugs except beer and in particular could barely look at Ronnie Finkell these days on the odd time he was around from wherever in the world he'd been posted. If Mark was going the same way I figured keeping in his good books was a smart move, more for Ronnie's sake. The amphetamine had him gripped and psychotic to high heaven at times; and no one knew exactly how he kept up all of the funding for his legendary consumption.

"Well, given I'm stealing more drugs than taking, I'll ring him."

Dr Baqri arrived and I buzzed her into the unit. She scanned the police form and in less than 5 minutes was kick-starting the admission. Colin and I shook hands as he left, promising to go for a beer when our shifts didn't clash.

***

I got off the bus on Mealhouse Lane the next morning,

walked down Flapper Fold Lane and waited outside the new police station on the corner opposite the fire station. It was better to talk face to face than to ring, so there was no record.

Mark got out of his car and did a double take as I beckoned him over the road.

His smile looked a little forced and I wondered if he was smart to me and Finkell regarding the stolen medication racket. I put it to the back of my mind. "Your cousin's been beat the hell out of. Face misshaped and puffed out. She won't press charges against the husband. It's not the first time."

"He's a complete prick. Gareth Fitzrover. Claiming unemployment but working on the side. Terrorises her. Had neighbours phoning in every other week with banging and shouting. All the families told her to leave. If she goes she's out of area in some shelter, there's nothing around her for ten miles. I can't do anything anyway unless she comes forward."

"I've seen this all before, working at the hospital. It'll only escalate. We're old friends. I can do something."

Mark looked briefly back at the cop shop then into my eyes. There was a hint of a nod. "I'll owe you one."

I tipped him a wink and walked home in the crisp April morning.

***

Woke around four in the afternoon, did two hours exercise to get the adrenaline flowing and wolfed down a steak with chips. Had a shower and dressed: Black Levi jeans, plain black sweatshirt, boots and my baggy leather jacket. Up the right sleeve I slipped my claw hammer and walked over Gareth Fitzrover's house, just near the bottom of Liscard Street adjacent the cemetery, as the sky turned black.

Saw the light on in the living room and the man himself shouting and gesticulating at the television. Took a good look around to make sure the street was empty, walked up to the door and rang the bell. Heard, "Who the fuck is this?"

He opened the front door and I stormed through, using the momentum of the inward swing to push him back onto the stairs. I raised the hammer and he flinched with his arms over his face.

"Shut your fucking mouth or you're dead."

He flapped his head on his neck. I indicated the living room with my thumb and followed him in. Shut the curtains at the bay window. "Sit down."

He put his hands up and said, "Take what you want."

"You like hitting women, son?"

His face froze and his eyes grew wide. Silence.

I jerked back my sleeve, letting him see the hammer in full. "You know who Lieutenant Chris Ferry is?"

His eyes shifted. I knew he'd heard the stories when I watched the blood drain from his face.

"Well, it's your lucky day. See, you'd already be rolled up in a carpet by now."

He looked at the hammer and covered his knee-caps.

"You don't get it. You need your legs. You've got twenty-four hours to fucking scarper. And if I hear you've laid a finger on another woman from Land's End to John o'Groats it won't be me standing in front of you. It'll be my mate. And he doesn't prat around. Do you understand?"

He took a deep breath, nodded and relaxed.

"So, you're going to pack your stuff, go to the bank and rent somewhere far away. Sell the house, give your missus half the money and get on with your life, aren't you?"

I darted forward and walloped him full force in the nose with the hammer. Blood spatter lashed the carpet.

"What? I didn't hear you."

He gurgled out a hissed confirmation.

"Good boy, Rover."

I hit him two or three more times and washed the claret off my leather jacket in the kitchen as he cleaned his face and packed his shit. We never spoke another word.

I left out of the back door, climbed the fence and walked down Liscard Street to Wigan Road. Had a couple of pints outside the Royal to settle my nerves, went home and slept all night.

***

Bethany Fitzrover nee Reed settled in well at the hospital, made friends with some of the other ladies and was surprised to find a letter offering her a divorce, an apology and half the house a couple of weeks later.

***

DS Mark Reed came and made us even on the last week of May when he persuaded the hospital that pressing theft charges against me would be ignored as a waste of money by the CPS. I'd been caught with twenty boxes of medications about my person on a routine search after they'd tightened up on stock checking since vast anomalies had been detected in the bean counting division. It stretched back years but they could only pin on me what was on my person that day. I said they were for personal use and nobody could prove otherwise.

He even pulled the fake arrest routine and escorted me off the premises as the patients pissed themselves laughing and cheered me as I was led away.

Gareth Fitzrover either told someone of my visit, or

else a neighbour may have seen me going in and I didn't realise. Maybe Mark spread the word. I didn't know and it didn't matter. But with my old career swished down the pan in disgrace, I was destitute and desperate. My professional reputation was in tatters because someone at the hospital leaked the story to the local press, kaiboshing any chance of proper employment. Rumours of Fitzrover's mashed face proved my salvation and I took the only labour I was offered: debt collection for a low level drug dealer. I knew the town backwards and with Ronnie as my eyes and ears too I was good at finding people.

The problem was it was too low-pay and too high-risk. I took thirty percent of the debt for a successful visit, but trying to negotiate with folks fucked up on drugs and without a pot to piss in was a straight up mug's game. So I decided I'd go legit. Hence, Gibfield Private Investigations, Market Street, Atherton Town, was born.

***

Up in the office on that Wednesday evening, as the sunset streaked purple above the red brick terraced skyline, I heard the rapping on the glass door at the bottom of the stairs.

Old Victor Barnes let Mrs Ricketts in and tried to ease her apprehensive expression with a warm smile and failed.

I hadn't even considered the fact that this line of work would potentially break a woman's heart and end a marriage. With me, I was used to healing hearts in the psychiatric hospital. I had a lot to learn.

He led her upstairs into my office which I'd decorated with a *Pulp Fiction* poster on one wall and Denzel Washington as Walter Mosley's Easy Rawlins in *Devil in a Blue Dress* on the other. I also had Michael Caine from *Get Carter* and the (still to this day stunning) Liz Hurley to lighten the ambience. Looking back, I can only explain the decor as a probable mid-life crisis, some kind of nostalgia trip to those hazy days way back when I first blue-tacked them up at university. I found them rolled up in a shoe box I'd forgotten I'd even kept, after my fiancée had packed my stuff before kicking me out after the sacking.

The rest of the office furniture consisted of a small desk and cheap computer chair.

I was about to say something laconic like "The man's been dipping his wick, lady," but thought better of it. I just nodded, went all British and said, "Sorry to be the bearer of bad news."

Mrs Ricketts looked stoic enough although a small tear did manage to escape her right eye. "Here's your money. Leave the pictures in the envelope, I don't want to see them."

I handed her the memory card I'd palmed in my fingers. "I thought I'd save you the visuals. It's a taped confession."

"What did you do? Beat it out of him?"

"What? No. I'll rough him up if you pay me some more money though."

"Good God no. Well, how…"

I took the memory card back and clipped it into the laptop and let the recording play.

Mrs Ricketts listened intently.

She said, "Is that Father Kay? My God," her mouth opened wide. "You bugged a confession booth you utter lunatic. That's despicable." She waited until the end of the recording then said, "What's a donk?"

I was telling myself, 'Jacob, you fall in love too easily', trying to ignore my perception of how pretty she was, and failing. "First time I've heard that as slang for a condom myself to be honest." Tried a smile. "What are you going to do?"

"Pack his bags the minute I get home. Kick his cheating backside out of the house."

"Best of luck. If you need me for anything, don't hesitate to call me," I said, trying to sound chivalric and not as desperate as I felt, but she was already out past the landing and clicking down the steps.

Old Victor Barnes locked the door behind her and moseyed up to the office with a bottle of rum and four pint cans of Carling Black Label. "Thought you'd want to christen your new headquarters."

I cracked open a beer and rinsed a tumbler I'd fetched out of the rest of the remnants of my whole working life: a large plastic container full of books, two pint glasses, said tumbler and three bags of clothes. Most of my wages over the years had gone on bills and renting, paying off other people's mortgages.

"Why not. Take the seat. Don't think I'm not working on finding who did for your window."

"If I was a younger man, I'd box them my own self," he grinned, "but you take care."

"Don't worry about me. I've got two of the craziest men in town on my speed dial. Also, I just want to say thank you for letting me rent here upstairs. Ever since the hospital thing I kind of get the feeling I need to prove myself all over again, you know what I mean?"

Since the story of my stealing pills got in the local paper all the jokers in town started saying stuff like, 'Well I heard of the Italian Job, but never the Olanzapine Job' and singing 'we are a self-medicating society' to the tune in the film. I got the gags and laughed along but I can't say I was never niggled by them. I'd gone from a respected clinician to a laughing-stock overnight, with full blown alkies who'd never done a day's graft in their lives taking the raw piss out of me to my face. The truth was I'd saved lives in my time there and it was a damn shame the thievery was all I'd be remembered for after all those years of doing my best for folks.

I owed Victor for sorting me out with the room above his shop. He was a good man from the Windrush Generation. One of the best nurses I'd ever worked with in all my years at the hospital was his niece, who came over maybe a decade after he did, and I'd be damned if a couple of racist dickheads chased him out of our Town.

"No sweat. There's a chance of redemption for everyone. Even you, young sticky fingers."

"Tell that to Father Kay. He's been out for my blood since nineteen ninety one. I might have pinched some pharmaceuticals but I sure as hell didn't rob a crucifix."

Victor chuckled. "Don't worry about Father Kay. He's just bitter since he put in for a transfer out of here ten years ago and they won't give him a bigger parish. So, who's ya back up?"

"Number one, my man gone rogue, Ronnie Finkell."

"Ronnie? The Hag Fold Hurricane? Former flyweight? He's Loco in Acapulco."

"That's him. He was a great boxer. The amphetamines got him. He tries to keep it together but he's fooling nobody. The business he's in, he knows the town like nobody else though."

Victor shook his head and let out a wheezy laugh. "Who else?"

"Lieutenant Chris Ferry, or Fez as he's known."

Victor's eyes widened, his brow narrowed and he whistled. "He's fucking dangerous man, what I've heard."

"If only half the stories about Fez are true, then everything's going to be alright old man. He never talks about anything, but rumour is he was recruited as some special black op elite soldier and seen service all over the world. He won't even tell me and I've known him since primary school. Your three balaclava boys don't stand a chance. Ronnie will know where to find them, and me and Fez will take care of the rest."

Victor kept his eyes locked on mine and tried to steady his hand as he sipped on his rum, but at the mention of the boy Fez I could tell he had a flash of his crazy grin that tremored from his mind's eye to his fingertips and he couldn't stop it from showing. He finally took a long swallow, bade me goodnight and headed off home.

When I was two pints sunk and alone with my mind I found my thoughts drifting back to the psychiatric hospital where I'd worked for ten long years. It wasn't the camaraderie from the team work, the banter, the feeling of connecting with people that I wished would come back to me to reminisce, but instead the cutting of ligatures from necks.

I'd see the ligature knife sliding slowly through the belts, strings, shards of clothes and even bin bags and seeing the blood rush back into those tortured faces.

Every now and then the shame of being caught with five hundred neuroleptics sellotaped to my torso in that snap inspection would intersperse, as would my girlfriend leaving me when the story hit the local paper, and Father Kay laughing in my face in the street the week afterwards. But I thought to myself, 'I saved over two hundred lives with that knife. Two hundred souls. They were paying me peanuts. What the fuck did they expect a fella from Atherton Town to do?'

My other habit I'd developed working in the hospital was the strategic use of mirrors to make sure nobody was following me. As I slouched backward and put my feet on the desk I clocked PC Chase in the mirror I'd screwed into the ceiling that angled onto Market street through the window behind my chair. I cracked open the window and shouted, "Stop bullying me, I can't afford to pay you any more bribes."

Chase looked up, laughed and used his lock pick to let himself in.

3

Relaxing in my chair I watched as my old mate walloped back the remaining four fingers of rum left by Victor while simultaneously cracking open a can with his other hand. He looked chinged up to fuck.

"So, what's Ronnie done to you that's got you chasing him around Athy park?"

"The twat sold me half a gram this morning. Bashed out a line on my dashboard and it nearly burned my nose off. It was sherbet dip mixed with baking soda he'd nicked out of Quality Save. I nearly crashed my bloody patrol car, the prick. Heard it on radio. He was in for five seconds, grabbed that and four packs of nineteen pence noodles."

I nearly choked as beer suds exploded out of my mouth. "Did you catch him?"

"No. Been up to his flat but he's not in."

"Maybe he wasn't answering."

"What I mean is I let myself in. I put a crack in his bong for taking the piss and had him off a tenner's phet. The strange thing was, there's a giant gnome in his living room."

"I heard he stole it from Tesco in revenge after they banned him for pinching cranberry juice."

"Yes, but the gnome had a spliff in its mouth and he'd left Babestation on for it."

"I can't explain that."

I knew if Ronnie wasn't home and he was riding the wave of a psychosis-inducing bender I knew where I'd find him. I wouldn't tell Colin and definitely not Mark. We were all old friends, but their jobs were their jobs after all. I needed the whereabouts of the balaclava clowns and Ronnie knew every clown in town. I didn't even know what I'd do when I got hold of them to be honest, so mates or not the cops were a no-no. In psychiatry, it was all about safe control, but in Atherton Town I was free to let loose. It actually scared me a little how much I was ready to rock and roll, but I can't say I wasn't enjoying it. I sat there, visualising using their balaclava'd heads like speedballs until Colin's guttural belch brought me back into the room.

"Reet, I've geet munchies. That whizz is burning a hole in my guts."

"It might not even be whizz."

He looked at me with a frown on his face. "What do you mean by that?"

"Ronnie likes to help people. If one of his customers looks depressed he'll cut up the phet with antidepressants. Or if they're psychotic he'll cut it up with neuroleptics. Without telling them."

"I don't believe this. I wondered why I was hungry."

"Have you never clicked on that Atherton has some of the fattest amphetamine addicts in the country?"

"Why?"

"Because there's hardly any speed in his wraps, like I said. I once saw him diagnose a buyer with a tension headache and chop up a Paracetamol combo."

"Unbelievable. I'm not having it, he does it for other people's benefits. He just keeps as much of it as he can for himself."

"How do you know he didn't sell you the sherbet dip because he saw you were tanning too much sniff?"

Colin just shook his head. "Bollocks. The cheeky cunt. Get the van."

He had me drive to:

Martin's Chippy next to Jr's for his fish

Mediterranean Fish Bar for their chips

and Bamboo House on Bag Lane for their curry, the fussy bastard.

I had a flashback of all us lads playing football on Wigan Road Park in the early nineties while I sat waiting for him in the van and Fez's face made me think. Then I knew why. I'd forgotten all about retrieving the bug that he'd lent me from Saint Richard's. I knew I had to get it back before the cleaners stumbled on it in the morn and Colin was too wired to pick the church door locks in the state he was in. I dropped him off at the cop shop car park and carried on up Flapper Fold Lane into Hag Fold and down to the scout-hut on Car Bank Street.

4

This place was usually packed by the Ju Jitsu club and amateur boxers, where Ronnie Finkell once shadowboxed in fact, but now as I entered it was near dark except for a circle of candles on the gym floor and Chris 'Fez' Ferry in his red kimono wielding a sword.

Not a wooden sword or knives like all the other trainers used. Oh no. A full blown samurai sword so sharp you could hear it swishing through the dust motes and chopping them in half.

He sprinted across the hall swinging the sword all around him and over to me before I could even shout his name. The blade landed squarely on my forehead and I could smell the steel.

He bowed and slid away the sword.

I smiled until I tasted the blood dripping down my face. "You've fucking cut me you crazy cunt."

"Testing your pain threshold. Only joking, I was a millimetre off. That's why I constantly practise. Discipline is the key. Let's have a look. It's only a nick."

As he was patching up the wound I tentatively explained that I'd forgot to retrieve the bug.

I think he felt a bit bad about gashing my head open and tried to swallow his anger.

"What you're implying, Jacob, is that we have to break into a church. You're supposed to be a private investigator not a tomb raider."

"What if Father Kay gives the bug to the cops or something?"

"Fair point. Is that old beggar still preaching?"

"More shouting than preaching really, but yes he's still in charge."

"I'd have preferred to practise my grenade throwing and garrotting techniques, but fair enough. We go in through the roof. I'll meet you on Mayfield Street at twenty three hundred hours."

"Roger."

He gave me the look. I tried a smile and shot down the fire escape.

On the way back to the office to get some street gear on I had an inspiration to lighten the mood and get Fez to loosen up. A bit of levity. Maybe even a lashing of light hearted revenge for slashing my head motivated me before I'd get down to the serious business of tracking Ronnie Finkell in the amphetamine hours of the morning. I had no idea it would turn out like it did.

***

Fez was already casing the church when I jogged down to Mayfield Street in the night air. He was dressed in what looked like a black jumpsuit, a ski mask and night vision goggles. I knew it was him when he gave me the grin like a wild shark. He had some type of abseiling kit hanging over his shoulders and looped around his waist.

I grinned back and gave him a thumbs up.

DS Mark Reed drove past us in his silver Merc, did a double take, shook his head and put his foot down.

Fez said, "I've been up and had a look. There's a skylight I can get through. Where's the bug?"

"In the confession booth."

"Tell me you're joking."

"Nope."

"Are you for real?"

"Yep."

"Have you no decorum? Bugging a confessional

booth?"

"I was doing my bit to save the planet."

He stared hard at me in disbelief. "I'm not lending you any more tools. You'll be desecrating graves next."

"Fuck off."

"Forget it. Concentrate on the job. All you have to do is ring my mobile if the lights go on in Father Kay's house behind the club. I'll be in and out in five minutes. Yes?"

I gave him the nod and watched him scale the wall. When he reached the roof I got my white sheet out of my bag and cracked two amber glow-sticks. Slipped the sheet on, put on a Freddy Kruger mask and tucked the sticks under the armpits.

I figured I'd wait till he'd dropped down into the alley, jump out and give him a laugh. What actually happened though was that on instinct I tried the handle of the front door and realised it was open. Giggling to myself, I sneaked into the booth, parted the curtain, climbed through the window and ducked down where Father Kay usually remonstrated. I could hear Fez zip-wiring about and bit down on my hand as the door creaked open. As soon as he stepped in and pocketed the bug I slung back the curtain and shouted, "You boy!" followed by some improvised cod Latin.

I was expecting him to laugh himself silly and jokingly rap me one in the ribs. He didn't. He dropped to his knees and cried, "May God forgive me!" Then he disappeared back up to the roof on his zip-wire.

I went outside, carefully closing the door. All I could make out was him running towards Hindsford, getting smaller and smaller in the moonlight, leaping from rooftop to rooftop like something from an old ninja film.

5

I went back to the office and waited for an hour for Fez to surface, to no avail. I reasoned that rather than hang around and waste the night talking to Liz Hurley I might as well make a start on the trail of the window smashers.

Given Colin had already scoped out Finkell's flat, located down a side street off Bolton Road, I knew instinctively he'd be holed up at his cousin's flat, Red Devil's, in one of the brown bricked two story blocks at the far end of the railway bridge.

He was nicknamed the Red Devil because he was once asked to renounce the devil by Father Kay in the run up to a christening, misheard what was said and shouted, "I'll never turn my back on Manchester United. How dare you." Sprinted straight out of the church. Never lived it down.

He was a minor heroin addict and as he let me in his eyelids drooped almost closed but he managed a greeting and a quick fist pump. "He's in the kitchen."

I hadn't been here in a while and was bemused by what I saw. The walls were plastered with press cuttings on the Manchester United teams from the nineties. One wall in particular was dedicated to the mercurial Frenchman, Eric Cantona, while another was like a shrine to Roy Keane. The entire ceiling displayed a collage of the European cup made up entirely of head shots of Sir Alex Ferguson.

Red Devil saw me looking. Shrugged and said, "Job centre don't give decorating grants anymore."

"Fair enough."

Ronnie 'Hag Fold Hurricane' Finkell was barefoot, about 7 stone piss wet through, did have the remnants of a dead cat for a belt and was staring intently at the radio trying to change the dial via telekinesis. The concentration he possessed was more impressive than the results.

Hag Fold estate, like a lot of council estates had a bad reputation that it didn't deserve. I'd lived there myself for a while with an old girlfriend and was struck by how close-knit the community was compared to some other parts of Atherton. The vast majority of the folks living there, along with the rest of the roughly twenty thousand inhabitants of the town, were mostly relaxing in front of the TV or already in bed after a hard day's work.

However, for the likes of Ronnie and the other phet freaks, crack heads, smack heads, car-jackers, joyriders, knicker sniffers, washing-line bandits, cat burglars, bare knuckle scrappers and even the odd wannabe pimp, it was more or less witching hour.

I took a beer from the Red Devil's fridge as Ronnie cooked a tea spoon, pulled back the syringe and injected the hot whizz into the vein on his hand.

There was a family in the ground floor flat waiting for a house and they'd left a kid's trampoline in the back. Some joker I didn't know kept bouncing on it and popping up at the window. Shouted:

"Red Devil"

Disappeared

Popped back up

"Can I borrow your bedsheets"

Disappeared

Popped back up

"For a parachute"

Disappeared

The fourth time he popped back up Ronnie grabbed him by the scruff off the neck and dragged him in.

"Get in you madman or someone will call the cops. What do you want?"

"Been to the mental hospital. They won't let me in.

They say I'm not crazy enough. I've had enough, Ronnie. I've been begging the GP for help for months. I'm going to teach them a lesson."

"What do you need a parachute for?"

"I'm going to jump off a multi-story car park so they know I'm serious."

"Well what do you need a parachute for then?"

"A safe landing. I'm suicidal but I need help with that. If I got no parachute I'll be dead and there's no help for that."

I knew from experience what the geezer was going through. With the trusts shrinking the inpatient bed numbers the criteria were strict for getting admitted to the hospital. We had folks trying to escape one way and folks trying to avoid being discharged the other way. Always at maximum capacity. Care in the community was a great idea in theory but there's only so much you can do for a person with daily pills and a weekly visit.

Ronnie disappeared and came back with a raggedy old fishing tent. "This should glide better than a cotton bedsheet."

I snatched the tent away. "Listen to me." And I told him exactly what to say next time he went back to the doctor. "But don't go overboard. If they think you're dangerous, you won't go to the acute unit of the infirmary, they'll lock you up in the Valley Lodge. That's medium secure and it'll take you a lot longer to get out of there."

"Didn't take me more than a month," Ronnie said.

"Because your psychosis was caused by drugs. Soon as they were out of your system you were fine. The Benny Big Bollock escapade. Remember?"

Ronnie rolled his eyes, shrugged his shoulders and shook his head. Red Devil was gouching in the corner on a bean bag and the suicidal geezer got comfy with a beer and a dab of speed. I wrapped a bit for myself in a Rizla and gulped it down. As I was thinking about it I wondered why it never pissed me off that Ronnie never remembered every time we bailed him out of the shit. I put it to the back of my mind and told the tale:

***

Was a Saturday night, quarter to twelve, above what's now a decent pub, Weaver's Rest. Opposite the sandstone obelisk. Back in the day it was called the King's Head. And upstairs there was an exclusive dance floor and dive bar for those in the know. And I mean dive bar. The kind of place you'd bang condoms on your fingers just to pick up your jar. The kind of place you weren't ashamed to be carried out of so you don't need to touch the floor. Loved it.

Nodded to the doorman, Simon 'Hairband' Braggins, who wasn't bald, he was just more evolved than the rest of us as he liked to say. I took his word for it. Swung open the pea green chipped wooden doors and floated through the blue grey plume of tobacco and ganja smoke that provided the interior's incense.

Squeezed through the swaying leather and linen to the bar. The frost of Black Label tingled my fingers. The shot of Jack Daniels hit my stomach with a sweet burn. The melody stroked my ears tenderly, a haunting lullaby from the stage.

Ford and the Shouts. Manchester Blues. She swirled serene euphony even the walls couldn't resist moving to. The guitarist strummed the acoustic's wire as deftly as a pervert on a nympho's g-string, reverberating nerve endings.

The staring eyeball scorched my awareness, slashing through the honeyed ambience like a vindictive switchblade. Benny Big Bollock. Singular. Sat in the corner with a peroxide blonde perched on each knee like they were guarding the crown jewel. Bold as brass right there in the boozer, the swollen extremity bulging over the unzipped flies making a certainty of his sobriquet as they took turns stroking his cock in time with the music. On the wrinkly scrotum was the tattoo of a wide eye.

Hoped I'd imagined it following me as I headed to Fez by the fruit machine.

"Took your time. Where's Finkell ended up then?" he mumbled, with a toothpick bobbing between his lips.

"The Valley Lodge. Straight from court."

"The Valley? What, the mental hospital?"

"Yes. Not just a mental hospital. A medium secure mental hospital. Fences like a Redwood Forest with razor wire as sharp as your shirt collar."

"For attempted robbery and unlawful imprisonment? Bit strange isn't it?"

"Not the only thing that was a bit strange. Just as the judge sentences him to a year in Strangeways, Ronnie shrugs off his suit jacket and rips his shirt wide open to the collar, fashioning a cape. Jumps out the dock and starts screaming about being Captain Council Estate, ridding the working classes of criminals and conmen. Orders the judge to lash himself in shame with his wig for daring to criminalize a modern day super-hero. Takes about ten bailiffs to pin him to the deck and drag him out as he's hollering righteous indignations. The judge reconsiders jail and orders a full psychiatric assessment at the Valley.

By the time I get there to see him, he's been chemically coshed and staring at me through the safety glass like a zombie in a paper gown. Blinked a bit and dribbled a lot."

"Thought it was funny him trying to rob the gasman. Lost the plot then, I take it?"

"Well this is where it gets even more strange. His version wasn't robbery. Apparently there was a dodgy scammer on the prowl who's turned up at an old dear's just down the road from his gaff. Claiming to be from British Gas. Goes in and cleans her out. Frightens her to death. Was in the paper. So, Ronnie, still paranoid schizo-wired from the drugs the night before, spies a van pull up outside and out jumps a gasman. Very convincing uniform he's thinking. No wonder the old mare let him in. Ronnie answers the door wearing nothing but a

smile and boxer shorts with his balls hanging out."

"His balls out?"

"Yes, to disorientate the conman apparently."

"He has lost the plot. Thought he was off the pointless powder?"

"I'll get to that in a minute. According to the gasman he's twigged that the guy's unstable but figuring it's only a quick boiler clean he'll just get it over with and against his better judgement goes in.

"As he's doing the mending, Ronnie jumps him from behind, hog ties him and drags him in the living room. The gasman, fearing he's going to get sodomized or worse, is pleading for Ronnie to check his identification and phone British Gas to confirm his identity, but he's having none of it.

"Apparently, because the gasman hasn't checked in with his dispatcher after such a small job, they give it twenty and alert the cops as a precaution.

"Meanwhile Ronnie's on the phone to one of the tabloids jabbering a hundred miles an hour with this Captain Council Estate Malarkey and claiming he's nabbed the fake. As he's negotiating an exclusive with a photo shoot, the police kick the door in and survey the scene. Ronnie's babbling that fast they can't tell a word he's saying as they're struggling to cuff him. In walks his mother with some shopping and Ronnie can't grasp why she goes ballistic on him, even when she's waving the note she left on the mantle-piece asking him to stay in because the gasman's due. No one's buying his story, taking him as gone loopy on the sniff."

"What a scene. Shouldn't laugh but it is funny. So why's he back on the drugs?" Fez said.

"He wasn't. Been clean for a while and holding down a job labouring and he was back in the boxing gym. He was however still in debt for them. A minor disagreement about accrued interest, and a certain exhibitionist and his pals pin him down and mainline this new super powder fresh from Columbia in his arm, completely uncut. To teach him a lesson. They were probably expecting it to kill him, but this

boy has handled more chemicals than Pfizer. Rode it physically, but as it's played out it was clearly too much for his pickle."

"Cheeky bastards."

"Exactly. Speaking of bastards, that's our cue. Thanks for tracking him, Fez, I owe you one."

"Not at all. My pleasure. Give Ronnie my best."

"Will do. Least he'll be off the drugs. Well the street drugs anyway."

We finished our pints with long swallows as Benny walked across the dancefloor with his shameless appendage bobbing around in front of him, leading the way like a divining rod heading to the toilets. Counted to ten and followed him in, Ford and the Shouts cruising to a mellifluent whisper as the door closed slowly behind us. He was at the middle urinal with his trousers round his ankles, grunting with strain to force piss through the erection. Fez waded up behind him as my boots sloshed atop the sodding floor. He slung a garrotte round Benny's neck with one hand and with the other fixed his pistol to the base of his bald skull gleaming with the fluorescent light.

"If that's what I think it is I suggest you remove it from the back of my head before I take it off you and make you eat it," Benny whispered.

"You haven't got the bollocks."

"Very original. Faggot are you?"

I took the hypodermic needle out of my pocket and flipped off the cap with the tip of my thumb. Lowered the plunger, shooting out a small spurt of cloudy liquid.

"Let me put it this way. Brace yourself. You're about to feel a sharp, hard prick. Uncut."

***

"Oh, yes," Ronnie said, "I remember now. Apart from the gasman thing and the court part. I wondered why my mam doesn't speak to me these days. Hang on a minute, that's why the Dremayne boys are after killing you. Benny Big Bollock Dremayne's no longer with us. Died in the Valley Lodge. Went even more mental than me when you injected him and never came out of it. Very nasty piece of work he was. Word on the grapevine is he had a heart attack mid-way through the act of trying to rape a nurse. They blame you and Fez for him being in there in the first place and they're going to string you up is what I heard."

"And you didn't think to tell me this before?"

"He only died last week."

"You've left me walking around for seven days?"

"A week isn't a long time up Hag Fold, pal."

"Not if you're whizzed up it's not. It is everywhere else."

"You're not really angry. It's the drugs talking. Relax and go with the chemicals. They're ambrosia for the brain stream."

Boxer or not I wanted to punch him hard in the face. "Why did they smash Victor Barnes' window?"

"To get at you. And also they're neo-fascists with very bad intentions."

"What?"

Ronnie shrugged and cooked up another spoonful. Red Devil was out cold and the suicidal geezer had found the gift of humour in our verbal sparring. I gave him a look and he necked his beer, saluted and said, "You lads proper cheer me up. Thanks for the advice. I'll go back to the doc's in the morning."

"Any time. Remember, no paragliding."

He laughed then dropped out of the window onto the trampoline. I heard a screech and looked out. The trampoline had collapsed on one side and he was face down, rolling in the grass. To this day I had no idea who he was and why he didn't just use the door.

6

If there was anyone in the world who didn't need worrying about it was the missing-in-action Lieutenant Chris Ferry. Still, I was worried. It was strange he hadn't at least sent a text. Then I checked my pockets and realised I hadn't even brought my phone with me.

The bad news about the neo-fascists with the sights on us skunked around my mind. The good news was if there were two more things Fez hated more than drugs and terrorist types I couldn't think of them.

I swallowed another few Rizla bombs of speed throughout the night and early morning and shot the shit with Ronnie for the first time in ages. With me working shifts our only interaction had been brief exchanges of cash, tablets and him passing on snippets of information in flying visits regarding trending pharmaceuticals for me to pinch.

"Don't you want to clean up and give the boxing one more chance before you're too old?"

"Not going to happen. It was a conspiracy. They rigged everything because they knew I'd move up in weight and beat Naseem Hamed."

"Come off it, man. I knew you were good but you'd never have even got near the Prince in his prime."

"Maybe it was the Prince who paid Benny to drug me out of fear."

I burst out laughing. "Your lady Polly Paranoia told you that? I heard they called you Powder Puff Gloves. Eight pro fights eight points wins. Where were the knockouts, Hurricane?" I tried to rile his pride a bit to plant a seed and it worked.

"Which pricks called me that? It's the sweet science I was known for, not the thuggery. And I was a scientist."

"Well why don't you ditch the chemistry and go back to your old science subject?"

Seeing his face in the flickering light of the TV I saw two expressions flip back and forth. One where the Hag Fold Hurricane was dying to jump up and lash out a fifteen punch combination and the other expression that was cold, calculating and was mainlined by the amphetamines.

I thought if I kept it up enough over time the boxing would win. Maybe instead of a dead cat for a belt he could be slinging the Lonsdale Belt around his waist.

Rather than keep bailing him out I felt I could be more proactive in helping him get back to his old self. Maybe the amphetamine dream would always win. I always had a feeling the driver of his present day monumental drug use was his failure at not hitting his potential as a pro. He'd picked up a torn bicep in his last fight and descended from recreational drug use down into the parallel life of full blown addiction. If I could get a trainer to take him on he still had a good three or four years in him. He was still lean, fit and in good shape from all the peddling on his bike and running around dodging debtors. He didn't drink or smoke and only kept the bong for nostalgia purposes, so I figured he had a chance. A plan formed in my mind on how to get his blood clean of the pointless powder.

In the meantime I matched him for what felt like half an ounce until two o'clock the following afternoon as Ronnie hooked up Red Devil's laptop and went through his playlist:

Naseem Hamed v Kevin Kelley

Don Curry v Lloyd Honeyghan

Both Nigel Benn V Chris Eubank fights

Ricky Hatton v Kostya Tszyu

Both Tyson Fury and Anthony Joshua v Wladimir Klitschko

Carl Froch's late stoppage win over Jermain Taylor

the greatest moments of Lennox Lewis, Frank Bruno and so many more I can't even remember.

Both our jaws ached from speed gurning, laughing and reminiscing about old times and I could see the boxing was definitely competing with the drugs in his blood.

I flicked on the news to re-orient to time and place and watched transfixed as some embassy in London had been hijacked. They were showing live feed and I could have sworn that hovering above the building, at the doors of the helicopter, was a man pulling on a ski mask and grinning a very familiar shark's grin. I rubbed my eyes and did a double take. It wasn't the drug drink cocktail. It was fucking Fez. He let loose what looked suspiciously like the abseiling kit he'd used the night before in the church as he descended to the embassy window ledge. I looked around to tell Ronnie but he was trying to change the channel with the power of telekinesis.

We went for a walk and ended up sat outside the old Pretoria pub, named after the old coal mine, on Spa Road. We used to drink there all the time and now it was boarded up and graffitied. It was a shame. Market Street had almost a dozen shiny new micro-pubs with cocktails and coloured gins and up here folks couldn't even get a decent pint any more. We cracked open some more cold Carling cans we'd got from the shop and enjoyed the afternoon sun.

"I need a top up. You coming?"

"No man, I'm flagging. Great to catch up though. Been too long. And think about the boxing. I'll help you out mate." It had been a long time since I'd joined Ronnie on a bender, especially as the world of work kept us all apart. With little hope knocking around, I could see how easy it could be to just keep on chasing that buzz; how easy to go under and embrace the never ending short-sighted hustle of chemical enslavement.

He laughed, threw some jabs and a hook and gave me a gummy grin. As he jogged off down the road I thought at least no one would be able to knock his teeth out. Because he had none left.

7

The chipboard window sobered me up as I passed it into the office. I had a full body wash and a shave in the sink, given I had only a toilet and no shower as yet. Slipped on some jeans and a blue cotton shirt and checked my phone. It was either the melancholy of loneliness or the chemical depression from the uppers leaving my system that made me phone the soon-to-be-former Mrs Ricketts.

I had no idea what I was going to say if she even picked up, which she didn't anyway. I didn't bother to leave a message and must have accidentally redialled with the fucking touchscreen fiddliness of these new phones. Give me an old Nokia with Snake on it anytime. One missed call I could have written off as an accident. Two looked like stalking and the queasy come-down jitters on top was a bad mix.

I needed food and didn't even have a toaster. Nipped to the post office to deposit half the cash from the Ricketts case. As I came out I saw PC Chase with a loudspeaker.

"Get off that roof before I come up there and give you the slapping of your life, pillock."

Couldn't help but laugh at his style. I'd negotiated people from rooftops at the hospital myself and almost volunteered to take over. Then I got a tactile hallucination of rattling pill boxes sellotaped to my legs and decided to watch.

At first I worried it was the geezer from Red Devil's the night before but I put my sunglasses on and saw there was no sign of a fishing tent parachute and I definitely didn't recognise him. It was some spindly geek waving his fists in the air.

He shouted, "As the last communist left in Britain, I declare a revolution, starting now. My first demand is that you reopen Atherton Town's job centre."

Colin replied, "What would you know about a job, you work shy twat. Get down now or I'll come up there and put your arm up your back."

"Listen to that, my fellow proletarians. This is what they think of us. They close down this very job centre and open up a funeral parlour right across the road!"

As the igniter of the revolution gesticulated to the new undertakers where the old Norweb used to be, he got a bit too fervent, slipped off the roof and his fall was broken by the V2 bus that was just about to pull out on its way to Manchester.

Colin was shaking his head as he moved in to check the guy's welfare. He saw me and shouted, "What do I do with him? Section 136?"

"You can't section people for their political views. That's what the communists did."

He burst out laughing and I saw two clear globules of coke remnants dripping down from his nose. He did the footballer snurch with each nostril as I doubled backed on myself to get something to eat to try and get rid of the burning feeling in my stomach.

I debated between the Corner House Café and The Snug. Decided on the latter to get off the main drag while I decided what to do now I was the hunted not the hunter, especially with Fez incommunicado for the time being. Cut down the cobbled alcove, ordered a coffee and a BLT and sat outside on the patio with a cigarette.

I was already jangly from the bad idea of tanning the speed last night and my nervous system went into overdrive when Mrs Ricketts came across the cobbles with a bag of shopping. Small town life in a nutshell.

I went all shy and tried to bury my face in a cloud of smoke but she recognised me instantly.

"Did Miami Vice ask for their suit back?"

She gave me a pearly white smile and I started to relax. "Very funny. Grab a chair. Can I get you something to eat?"

"Just a coffee. No sugar."

Tried, rather pathetically, "I bet you're sweet enough."

"I'm a type two diabetic."

"Oh."

I brought her drink and tucked into the sandwich they'd handed me over the counter.

"So, what do I call you?"

"Ms Katherine Porter. Katy is fine."

"You've got rid of the Ricketts already. That was quick."

"Been straight to the solicitors today to get the divorce papers rolling. It'll take some time but I'm not messing about. Life's too short to waste, don't you think?"

"Did he admit to the affair?"

"He denied it at first but I told him I knew for a fact and that if he was telling the truth he had to swear to God. He just broke down after that. Did the usual: said it was a mistake, begged for forgiveness, told me that he'd change and it was just a fling, meaningless sex. Like I say, the usual. I just told him to pack his things and go. Already phoned to get the locks changed next week." She sipped on her drink as I listened, admiring her grit.

I thought about it and I was glad he did admit it. It suddenly hit me how monumentally stupid and if truth be told, lazy, I'd been to bug the church. If he'd denied it, could the bugged conversation have been used as evidence in a divorce proceeding? Was it a crime to bug a confessional booth? I had no idea. I figured I'd find an excuse to call to her house one day and get the memory card back and destroy the evidence just in case. It happened quicker than I thought.

I said, "*Ne nuntium necare*," trying to pull the sophisticated, educated look.

"I beg your pardon?"

"Don't kill the messenger. It's Latin."

"Why don't you just speak English?"

"Never mind. I just meant don't taint me as a harbinger of bad news."

"I know. I'm just teasing you."

"Oh."

"I'm glad you just confirmed what I'd thought. Our marriage had probably been dead for a good while. We haven't slept in the same bed for over a year."

"OK."

"Too much information?" she grinned.

"It's quite hard to shock me to be honest."

"Good. Let's go back to my house and fuck. Shocked?"

"Touché," I said. Indeed I was.

We got in her car parked near the front of the Subway on Eckersley Precinct and cruised to her house on Tyldesley Road. While we were driving the conversation went like this:

"Talk about speed dating," I said

"I'm free and single. What did you want? To be romanced?"

"A bit of poetry wouldn't have gone amiss."

She looked over, rubbed my crotch and laughed.

We started on the kitchen table, moved to the couch and ended up upstairs walloping the bedsprings. By the end of the couple of hours my back was giving out and her make-up was smudged all over the show. Her neat, light brown curls framed her breasts as we lay facing each other catching our breath.

"I think we both needed that," I said.

She smiled. "It certainly appeared so. I hope you don't think I'm being presumptuous but you know there's nothing in this. I don't want to lead you on into any kind of relationship or anything. I'm not even divorced yet."

"Don't worry, I feel the same. I'm not long out of a relationship myself." What I really felt was that I should tell her I fell for her on first sight. I understood what she was saying though and it did both of us good; we'd belonged to someone else and we had to get it out of our systems that we were free to do as we wanted, to forget lamenting for dead relationships. If the truth be told, did I feel used? *Most definitely.* Was I complaining? *Was I fuck.*

She climbed out of bed and I admired the view as she walked to the *en suite* shower.

She flicked her hair back and said, "Are you coming?"

"In a minute. I'm just trying to get the blood back in my head."

As soon as the water flowed I went over to her laptop, popped the memory card out and stuffed it in my jeans pocket. Then I joined her in the shower, kissed the back of her neck and we went at it again with soap suds flooding everywhere.

We got dressed and flipped coins for something to eat. She won and fancied some pub grub. Drove us down to the Talbot on Wigan Road. We sat outside with a pint and some wine in the summer evening. I rattled through a rump steak and chips lashed with peppercorn sauce and Katy had the sirloin with salad.

My mate Dean Robinson was on his way out of the beer garden. He raised his eye brows at my company and gave me the grin that said, '*you've done alreet there mon.*' Necked the rest of his pint and said, "How's tricks?"

"New business. I'm a P.I."

He chuckled and shook his head.

"I'm serious. If I ever need a driver do you fancy earning a bit of cash in hand?"

"No probs. You've got my number."

"Before you go, have you seen a blue Fiesta with or without plates driving about round town?"

He shook his head.

"Ever heard of Benny Dremayne?"

"Who?"

"Neo-fascists?"

"In Athy?"

"Never mind. Good to see you mate."

He left and I turned my attention back to Katy. We did the comfortable small talk, even more comfortable silences and relaxed together for a few hours.

She dropped me at the office around eight o'clock and we even kissed goodbye.

Even though I mourned nothing more would come of it I enjoyed being back in the dating game, if you could call what we got up to a date. She said she'd call me sometime and I didn't believe her.

8

Victor was sat in his barber chair seemingly lost in thought and sipping a drink when I let myself in.

"Evening my friend. You aren't still worried about the window are you?"

"No man, I'm just planning on redecorating the entire shop. It was a shame the brick smashed not just the window but those old mirrors eh?"

"Well I've got some good news and bad news. The good news is they smashed your shop largely because of me. They're after my neck."

"That is good news," he said with a wide grin.

"The bad news is apparently they're neo-fascists which is why they picked you to get at me."

"In Atherton Town?"

"Exactly. The good news is that I don't have to waste time tracking them. Because the bad news is they want me and Fez's blood."

"Which is bad news for them right?"

"It would be if I knew where Fez was. I think I saw him on a zip-wire on TV and haven't heard from him since."

"A zip-wire?"

"Never mind. All I'm saying is I'm sorry about this mess. Don't worry, I'll sort it."

He rolled up the trouser on his left leg to reveal a holster and a small revolver. "I'm not worried, man. Back in the old country we don't fuck around."

"Good lad."

In the office upstairs I checked my phone and realised it had gone dead so slung it on charge. Eventually it came back on and I'd hoped there'd be a *goodnight* or something from Katy but there was nothing. Not a message or missed call from anyone. After the Katy episode it really did click to me how lonely I was. How lonely this business was. I'd been part of a forty person team for ten years and now here I was looking at Denzel as Easy and Uma as Mia Wallace on the walls for company. Tried my best to resist some small talk with Liz Hurley. I'd had a fair chunk of speed the other night and I had no idea how I'd react if things got trippy and she talked back to me.

I had no contacts in the DVLA to help with the Fiesta full of clowns and when I flicked through my phone had almost no contacts anyway. I was *persona non grata* at the hospital and I couldn't blame my ex-colleagues from keeping their distance. I'd thought about social media for the business but I was old school in wanting word of mouth. Less easy to be stung in a trap by Benny's revenge merchants. I thought about getting tooled up like Victor myself but figured my claw hammer and Fez would be enough.

My big mistake was fucking about the following day trying to think through a plan of action to no avail, as my thoughts were rushing with the last remnants of a drug hangover and a fair bit of moping. I reasoned it'd be a good idea to calm down my mind so I popped a couple of benzos and a couple of neuroleptics washed down with some Carling. I miscalculated the dosages and slept for about 17 hours. Had a wash and ignored the phone. I reckoned I'd let Katy make the next move, if there was to be a next move that was.

I got claustrophobic in those four walls and couldn't face another night talking to posters so with the sky still light I did what everyone did who was at a loose end on a Friday afternoon, had cash in their pockets and people out to string them up:

Decided to go out and get pissed.

A text vibrated just before I was about to leave. Was

PC Colin Chase. Said: *Pint?*

    Great minds as they say.

    The second mistake I'd made was accidentally knocking the phone onto silent and not checking it properly. I only saw Colin's text because of the noise as it rattled on the desk.

9

I'd met Colin on the corner junction of Flapper Fold Lane and Mealhouse Lane outside the Rami Indian restaurant. He'd showered and changed out of uniform at the station.

He said, "Shall we call on Si?"

I was supposed to be the detective and it hadn't even occurred to me to follow up with Si 'Hairband' Braggins to check if anybody had talked to him about that night with Benny Big Bollock back in the day. The way I saw it there was only really him who'd remember. I couldn't picture any of the other patrons from back then being able to place us. But if I could find out who'd been asking around I could work backwards from there and find them before they found me. Ronnie Finkell had said he knew of them but not where they lived.

Simon was anther of our childhood football pals and had been a bouncer since he was eighteen. Was a fourth degree Ju Jitsu black belt. I hadn't seen him on the doors in a while and wondered what he was up to for money these days.

"No idea what he's doing," Colin said, as we walked up Bolton Road passing Houghton Homes on the right. We turned left across the street from I&S newsagents where the bookmaker was and went down Car Bank Street to Si's.

Up the path we saw the entire front living room window was blacked out with what looked like a purple curtain. We exchanged glances and shrugged.

Colin indicated for me to duck in behind him, banged on the door with a grin on his face. Shouted, "It's the police. Open this door now."

We saw the curtain twitch and then the door swung open. Simon poked his head out with an alarmed air about his person. He was dressed in a gas mask, a leather thong and what appeared to be melted candle wax all over his hands.

"It's all consensual, officer. Who's called the police? There must be some mistake."

Colin pissed himself laughing. "What the fuck are you up to?"

I looked over Simon's shoulder and said, "That's not a sheep is it?"

"You two dickheads," Si said. "What do you want? And no, it's not a sheep, it's my rug. I've got it on a maiden while it dries. I spilt massage oil on it. Had enough of the doors. I'm a gigolo."

Colin was rolling on the floor struggling to breathe just at the same time DS Mark Reed drove down the street in his silver Merc. He did a double take, shook his head and put his foot down, speeding on by.

A woman's voice shouted, "Whip me, loverboy."

"One second, petal," Si replied.

"Can I ask you a quick question?" I said.

"The answer's no. I heard Benny snuffed it and expected either you or Fez to come knocking. Nobody's come near me mate. If anyone does I'll bell you."

"Thanks pal. We're going for a pint if you fancy it?"

Colin got back up, composed himself, took in the gas mask again and burst out laughing. Si slammed the door shut.

We retraced our footsteps and went in the Players Lounge as the first stop. Had a couple of games of darts.

"Don't take this the wrong way mate," I said, "but you're heavy on the piss water and sniff. Everything ok?"

"Three simple words. The job's fucked."

"Fair enough."

We worked our way down town, pub crawling it through:

Red Lion

Weaver's Rest
The Lamp
The Casba
Jolly Nailor
Mountain Dew
Pendle Witch
Wheatsheaf

And ended up in The Mill where we drank till closing time, too pissed to go to any other pubs. Colin had got hold of some of the white stuff somewhere along the way and I vaguely remember leaving him to it.

I don't remember collapsing on the floor of my office or pissing and puking all over the show.

I do remember the morning after though very clearly – when DS Mark Reed and a couple of uniforms I didn't know arrested me for the murder of Mrs Katherine Ricketts.

10

They cuffed me and put me in the back of Mark's car.

He said, "The bloody state of you. You dare be sick."

Drove to Atherton station and they put me in the holding cell, leaving me to stew in last night's sweat. I was shaken up to high heaven and had one of those hangover headaches where you feel you've been lobotomized with a rusty ice pick. My eyes stung and I was numb with shock.

Mark came in and looked puzzled. Said, "Before we start, can I just ask why Si was dressed like that?"

"Mate, to be honest, my throat's as dry as Ghandi's flip-flops, I've just found out the latest love of my life is dead and you've arrested me over her murder. Si's apparel is the least of my worries."

"I suppose so. I just can't get the gas mask out of my head."

I freaked out. "Fuck the fucking gas mask. What the fuck is going on?"

"Oh right. Where were we? That's it. Mrs K Ricketts has been pronounced dead."

"How?"

"I'm not telling you."

"Why not."

"Because you might slip up and reveal more than you're supposed to know."

"Oh fuck off, Mark. I've known you for thirty years. You know I'm not a murderer."

"Thought it was a bit strange but in this job you just never know. We have to bring you in even if it's just to eliminate you from our enquiries anyway."

"But you're drug squad."

"I know but we're short staffed. Murder squad are

rushed off their feet all over Greater Manchester. Also, they know I know you, so I pulled some strings which to be honest is shining me in a bad light after the stolen medication escapade. I'm not saying I suspect you. But I am saying you were the last person seen with her. Half the Talbot saw you eating together and half of Tyldesley Road heard you shagging her. Where were you on Thursday night?"

I thought about lying. Ruled out Finkell to make up an alibi because he wasn't a credible witness. Couldn't ask Colin and I had no phone to tip anyone else off. I started to worry and panicked about being one of those miscarriages of justice you see on the TV. Also, I was absolutely devastated that Katy had been murdered. Just couldn't believe it. Decided the truth was the only thing to go with.

"In my office above the barbers." Passed out because of self-pity.

"What office."

"I've opened up a private investigation company."

"You've done what? I just don't believe this. Shagging your customers? Where's your service ethics?"

"She came on to *me*."

He stood there shaking his head. Said, "Well your fingerprints are all over the place and obviously there'll be DNA."

"You haven't got my fingerprints."

"I know. It's part of the script to intimidate and make you confess."

"I clearly have nothing to confess. I was in love with her."

"Alright. I'll see if I can get you some scran and a bottle of water. When I come back though it's going to have to be a conversation on tape." He headed for the door.

I had a quick thought. "Mate, before you go. Just out of curiosity, is there a problem if someone hypothetically like bugged a church or something like that?"

"I'm going to pretend I haven't heard that Jacob."

As he closed the cell door it quickly re-opened. PC Chase came in looking as rough as me. Said, "Here, have an eye opener," offering a bag of coke.

"Thanks mate but I don't think that's the best idea given the circumstances do you?"

"Don't worry. We'll get whichever cunt did it."

"Cheers man."

His radio went off:

Fire. Barber Shop
Market Street
Urgent
Perpetrator disappeared on foot

"Shit, Mark's coming back. Stash this for me." He threw the baggy.

"Are you taking the piss? I'm arrested for murder. I'm sat in a police cell. What if he strip searches me?"

"You'll only get done for possession." Then he flew down the corridor.

Well that just topped off the week really. My lover murdered and the man who took me in after I'd got sacked from the hospital had his windows put through and now his shop set on fire. Add to that a bag of someone else's class A drugs down my underpants in a police station. Me being falsely accused of the murder. I can only describe being on the borderline of psychosis. That just about summed it up along with the panic. And fear. Until I heard, *'no casualties in the barbers thank fuck'* in the corridor then it went straight back to plain old insanity.

I sat there for two hours waiting for Mark to come back with his tape deck, thought *fuck it* and waxed some of Colin's coke. Had a chat with Liz Hurley who was talking to me through the walls. It was a weird feeling to go from the hunter to the hunted and I'd just had about enough of looking over my shoulder. The coke kicked the paranoia off bad style and all I could smell was Katy's perfume. I felt like a rabid animal but focused on Liz's voice to try and keep from crying as I lost track of time.

After what felt like half a day, Mark finally swung the door open. His face looked grim. He sat down with the tape recorder and clicked it on, formally announcing the date and time.

"This is Detective Sergeant Mark Reed interviewing the suspect, Jacob Gibfield."

I shit myself.

"Now Jacob. What went through your mind after your murderous instincts took over and you lost control?"

"Mark, what the fuck are you on about?"

He clicked the tape off and said, "You should see your face. You're free to go. I'm not supposed to say, so keep it to yourself, but Thursday night Mr Ricketts must have snapped when he'd heard about you two. He smothered his wife with a pillow, probably in the early morning. It was him who burned down Victor Barnes' shop a few hours back because he thought it was your office, not realising your place was upstairs. It's a proper tragedy. He went straight to Father Kay to confess but the priest told him to come back next Wednesday for confession. He clearly couldn't wait and strung himself up from the scaffolding across the road. On his suit lapel he'd clipped a note that said *JUDAS PRIEST* and in his pocket he'd wrote a signed confession giving details only the killer could know."

My hands shook as all sorts of thoughts went through my head. I just couldn't believe all this had happened. I'd only been open for a week. "Thanks for letting me know pal," was all I could muster.

"I haven't finished yet and there's no easy way to say

this. We had to go through your phone. She rang you four times before she passed away. Probably in a panic and for help."

Fucking great. A tsunami of unadulterated guilt ripped through my bloodstream and flattened the coke clean out of my system. I leaned forward with my head in my hands. Even Liz Hurley fucked off.

"There's something else you need to do."

"Top myself?"

"Look, just calm down. Don't go blaming yourself. Anyway, there's a turn up for the books. Fez needs your help. He texted you to say he's checked himself into the mental hospital and he wants you to visit him later."

I couldn't believe what I was hearing. "What the fuck?"

"The text says he's had some kind of spiritual awakening and he's questioning his life's work."

"He hasn't had a spiritual awakening."

"How do you know?"

"Is all this off the record."

"Within reason."

I explained about the mask and the glow-sticks. Mark did a couple of double takes and shook his head. Then cracked into hysterics. Said, "He'll fucking kill you."

"He'll have to join the queue."

I came out of the cop shop dazed and in the throes of full blown mental breakdown. Figured I'd try and walk it off and took the scenic route. Headed up Gloucester Street and looked to my left across the fields separating Meadowbank and St. Richard's primary school, the latter being my first place of learning. I wondered why life couldn't be as simple as it was way back then.

I was lost in rose tinted daydreams of football at playtime, kiss-chase, playing British bulldog and whatever else and tried to work out how Fez was going to react when I explained the prank. Didn't see the blue Fiesta until the very last second.

11

I braced myself and managed to roll onto the bonnet of the car after it weaved from the wrong side of the road and came straight at me. I glided up onto the roof and somehow clung on until they hit the brakes. Slid down and hit the pavement. Couldn't believe I wasn't seriously injured.

Two blokes clambered out the front and the third popped the boot, all in balaclavas. They tried to drag me round the back of the car and instinct kicked in.

I used my breakaway technique to shrug off the guy gripping me from behind and lashed out at the man in front, connecting with a haymaker to his temple. I swung again and missed and got one on back the forehead. The one behind me took my legs and I hit the tarmac.

They were busy bundling me in the boot when luck, whether I felt I deserved it or not, played out in the shape of Dean Robinson's work van.

He leaned hard on his horn and drove the van into the side of the Fiesta, spinning the car to a right angle on the pavement. I rolled out of the boot and scrambled away. The balaclava boys scattered like ten pins and clambered back into their vehicle. The driver wound down his window and said, "Live in fear you fucking cunt."

"You don't know the half of it, arsehole," I shouted back.

What made it worse was this palaver was going on only two hundred yards from the bastard police station.

They sped off and I jumped into Dean's passenger seat.

He tried to keep the smirk off his face and said, "Your new career seems to be quite colourful."

I thought colourful was a fair choice of word. "Take

me to the psychiatric hospital."

He cracked. "Checking yourself in?"

Shook my head. "They probably wouldn't have me in there one way or the other."

12

It was only when we'd reached the car park of the hospital that my wits had returned enough to actually thank Dean for saving my arse. I promised to pay to repair the dent in the van's front and he gave me a wave as he headed home.

I think I was mostly on autopilot as I gingerly made my way through the automatic lobby doors and rang the doorbell on the men's unit.

A burly nursing assistant I vaguely knew gave me a grin. Shouted up the corridor, "Lock the medicine cabinets, the psychiatric Ronnie Biggs is back."

Felt like punching his fucking lights out. "I'm visiting. Mr Chris Ferry, please."

He beeped me through the second set of doors and led me to the dining area that doubled as the visiting space. I looked over at the lounge and couldn't believe my eyes.

Father Kay was perched on the edge of a green faux leather settee and staring out of the window with what I could only describe as a lost look on his face. All I needed. More guilt. I switched tables out of his eye-line and tried to calm down.

Fez came a couple of minutes later with two hot cups of tea. He looked as relaxed as I'd ever seen him in my life. His smile was slack and easy and his eyes were bright now that he wasn't always scowling.

He said, "I really appreciate you visiting, mate."

"I forgot to get you some grapes. Been a busy day."

"Why, what's happened?"

I filled him in on my arrest, the murder-suicide and the attempted kidnapping.

He said, "So that's why Father Kay checked himself in."

"He's a patient? I thought he was spreading the Gospel or something."

"He must blame himself. You've got to tell him about the bug."

"He'll go fucking ballistic. Can't you tell him?"

"Jacob, this is your mess. It's imperative for your own soul that you sort this out yourself. Search for your own atonement."

Imperative? Soul? Atonement? *What meds had they given this fucker*, I thought.

"What do these balaclava boys want with you?" he said.

"Benny Big Bollock died in the Valley Lodge. Supposed to have had a heart attack trying to rape a nurse. His crew reckon it was our fault that he was locked up in there in the first place. And it's not just me they want, it's you too."

"You injected him so why do they want me?"

"You put the gun to his skull."

"Yes, I suppose. Well, I won't resist them. If they want their pound of flesh I'll just let them take it."

I couldn't believe my ears. Managed, "They're neo-fascists. They targeted old Victor Barnes too."

He frowned and said, "In that case I can definitely see it tilts the moral scale a tad."

"Moral scale?"

"That's exactly why I'm here, Jacob. See, I had a spiritual awakening in the church that Wednesday night. I saw something. It may have even been an angel. I got called away the night after and tried to ignore it, but I've had time to think about all the violence. I've took a week's leave and I came here for professional help regarding my way of life."

I did the empathetic nod and tried hard to mirror his relaxed body posture. "You couldn't do me another cup of tea could you, mate?"

"Course."

While he was away I went to the comedian nursing assistant. Said, "I'm going to break some bad news. His beloved cat has just been found dead and I'm not sure how he's going to react when I get to telling him. Can you alert the rest of the staff that there might be a situation in a few moments? I'd probably call the psychiatric emergency team too, just to be on the safe side."

He looked puzzled. "He's been a model patient."

"He loved that cat like nothing else. And he's highly trained in every fighting code in the world. Trust me. I can sense sometimes when things might kick off. You know I used to work here."

It was the mention of the martial arts that got the fella to round up the cavalry. They did the old thing of surrounding the room and trying to look innocuous, carrying empty ring binders and clipboards or watering plants. Fez didn't even notice.

"There you go mate. One sugar."

"Thank you. You know this potential angel?"

"Yes."

"Did you see its face?"

"No. I had my infrared's on. Could just make out this weird glow. I can't believe how much at peace I felt in every fibre of my being. It touched me deep in a place I never even knew I had."

"The thing is if you'd have looked properly you'd have seen a Freddy Kruger mask."

"Beg Pardon?"

"And a white sheet."

"Sorry?"

"And two glow-sticks."

"How so?"

"Because it was me underneath the mask."
"Come again."
"A prank. A jape. Light-hearted banter."
"How interesting."

I kicked back the chair and made a run for it. He flipped over the table and cried, "You're fucking dead, Jacob Gibfield!"

The psychiatric staff had him surrounded. I headed for the doors and tried to get someone to let me out. Listened in to the commotion. Went as follows:

Nurse: Please calm yourself down. Don't take your grief out on the furniture.

Fez: Grief?

Nurse: We've all lost pets, Mr Ferry. We have some nurses trained in bereavement counselling to help you. Please just calm down.

Fez: What cat? There's clearly some misunderstanding. I want to discharge myself.

Nurse: I can't let you go home in such an agitated state. If you try to leave I'm afraid we have the power to keep you here.

Fez: It's all Jacob's fault.

Nurse: Don't go blaming your friends. Now will you calm down and agree to at least stay the night until you're settled or do we have to section you?

Fez: Section me? Oh, wait till I get my hands on him. Fucking glow-sticks?

(He threw a chair at the window at this point)

Nurse: If you don't calm yourself we'll have to give you something to help you calm down.

Fez: What do you mean?

Nurse: You either swallow some tablets or we'll inject you.

Fez: Like fuck you will.

Nurse: Calm down of your own volition then, Mr Ferry. Sit down with me and we'll talk it through.

The nurse did her de-escalation perfectly and he slumped in a chair next to Father Kay, who I saw hadn't even batted an eyelash at the commotion.

Someone in a uniform buzzed me out and as I slunked down the stairs I bumped into Doctor Gupta. He said, "Well hello, Jacob. I'd shake your hand but I'm frightened you'll snatch my watch."

Everyone's a fucking comedian. He was a great psychiatrist though and listened throughout my explanation of the Fez situation. I managed to get him to agree to let him go as soon as he was calm. Despite my thievery he had respected my judgement and skills over the years, and at least he saw the humour in the prank, unlike a certain Mr Ferry. The last thing I needed was him blaming me for being injected and put in a seclusion room.

I felt terrible about the impact of the Ricketts murder-suicide that Father Kay must have thought was somehow his fault. I knew that sometime soon I'd have to confess. But I just couldn't do it today. There were too many people on my case already.

13

I caught the bus back home and jumped off across from the Punchbowl pub around seven. Went in, got a pint and stood outside the front entrance on Market Street trying to light the smoke in my shaking fingers. The mind games from the balaclava boys were working exactly as they'd intended. I was checking every car that cruised down the road.

I think it was the idea of safety in numbers that got me to check the local paper back in the bar for the local football to see if there was a game on because I figured I'd be a sitting duck on my own in the office. Atherton Town, Atherton Collieries and Atherton Laburnum Rovers had already played in the afternoon, so I checked the rugby league listings and struck lucky as the Leigh Centurions had an evening kick-off.

I decided against a taxi in the vain hope the walk would burn off the previous few days' events and help me clear my mind so I could formulate a plan. I walked down Wigan Road and turned left at the Talbot, heading along the grass verge by the side of the Atherleigh Way bypass all the way down, passing the Parsonage retail park on my right and crossing the roundabout and over the bridge where Leigh East was on the left.

As I entered the Leigh Sports Village complex I had the grand total sum of sweet fuck all in the ideas bank. I was burning out. So much for the therapeutic power of walking.

Paid at the gate and sat in the West Stand, feeling at least relatively safer with the red and white wall of noise coming from the standing terrace of the North end.

I sat back and settled in to watch the beautiful and brutal ballet only the Great Game of Rugby League can offer, mesmerised by the sheer ferocity, intensity and flair on the field.

Lost in the action of the match I almost didn't register another old mate from Atherton Town, Sykes, two rows down, until just before half time.

He was drinking a pint and looked preoccupied, half-cut and red-eyed to fuck. I gave him a nudge. "You're miles away."

"I'm back writing."

"Makes sense."

"How's tricks?"

I told him all of it in the half time break, hoping he could help me think things through. He was a student of psychotherapy and he kept the perfect poker face all the way through, even though I sensed he was struggling to hold back from cracking up. Until I got to the murder-suicide.

"You blame yourself."

"It was my fault."

"Given Katy suspected the affair, isn't it plausible she would have eventually found concrete proof, like a love letter or developing an STD?"

"OK."

"Then she would have kicked him out."

"Right."

"Then she'd have moved on and he would plausibly have snapped anyway, just maybe at a later date, right?"

"Fair point."

"Ergo, although you may well have accelerated her harrowing plight, you are not totally responsible, yes?"

Sense and perspective were exactly what I needed and for the first time in as long as I can remember I began calming down a bit.

"What should I do about Benny Big Bollock's cronies?"

"Get Fez back on side and call them out publicly.

Target their macho pride. Otherwise you'll be looking over your shoulder until it suits them. Strike first and strike hard."

"Easier said than done."

"He's your mate. He'll forgive you at some stage. That's what old mates do."

"Will you talk to him for me?"

"How angry is he?"

"Let's say he's a tad miffed."

"Well you can fuck that, you're on your own."

I pondered what he'd said as the second half flew by. It made sense. There was no way I could keep on creeping around being afraid of being kidnapped again and I figured out a way of drawing the fuckers out into the open. I still couldn't get Katy out of my head, but the horror I felt at the tragedy of her death I tried hard to channel into a more useful emotion: anger.

After the game we shared a taxi back to town.

Sykes said, "Did I tell you about the time I shook Queen Elizabeth the Second's hand when Her Majesty came to open the stadium?"

"On May the Twenty First Two Thousand and Nine. Yes. Yes you have."

He went on to tap the taxi driver on the shoulder and tell him. I could have sworn the taxi man rolled his eyes and I suspected even *he* had heard it before. It was ten years ago but Sykes never failed to shoehorn the story into almost every conversation since, to the point I knew it by rote.

We got the cab to drop us off outside the Mountain Dew for the traditional *Dew Till Two* booze spree. Sykes lost an arm-wrestle in a pathetic four seconds against local cage fighter out of the Blackledge gym, Paul 'Pitbull' Horrocks.

Bethany, Mark's cousin, nudged me as I was laughing at the one-sided contest.

"Can I get you a drink? I owe you one," she said.

I normally would have gallantly declined but I was running low on cash and accruing more debts than cases. "If you insist, I'll have a pint."

She brought the drinks back to the table. Said, "Mark told me you had a hand in helping me out. I just wanted to say thank you. That bastard had me hostage for years."

She looked great. Her face had healed and there was a spark in her eyes that cheered me up no end. Maybe it was the drink, but I realised I had done some good in the midst of the chaos that was my current predicament. Along with my expertise with the ligature knife back in the day I started to feel a bit more myself. That was until one Mr Chris Ferry stomped into the pub and leaned over the table as the hairs on my neck stood up.

14

I tensed and braced myself for the barrage of blows that never came. He leaned over and hissed, "Get me a beer. I believe I have a dead cat to mourn."

Relief flooded through me as I staggered to the bar more in shock than anything else. I'd expected a hiding of a lifetime but obviously I'd underestimated our friendship. Maybe he finally saw the humour after having a few hours to calm down. Whatever it was, I let it lie and drilled into my head not to mention any of it ever again, even in jest.

We went out into the back, lit some cigarettes and sat down in the cooling night air.

"I've cancelled my leave and I'm back on call so we need to sort these fuckers out ASAP," he said.

"Well I've asked around and nobody knows where they live."

"Types of stuff they're into, they won't be listed on the electoral register will they? What they usually do is pay people to use their names for flats and houses so they're off the grid. What do you suggest?"

"I'm going to plant a sarcastic obituary in the *Atherton Telegraph, Leigh Reporter and the Journal* first thing on Monday morning. Draw them right where we want them. Then we sort this shit once and for all."

He grinned the shark's grin and nodded along.

We walloped back the beers in the raucous atmosphere of the pub, chatting away to all the faces of Old Atherton Town and as we waited for a kebab next door I forgot myself and said, "Sorry the prank went a bit wrong."

His face flickered for a millisecond then he smiled and did the strangest thing he'd ever done in all the years I'd known him. He gave me a man hug. He gripped me quite tight and I felt a vague tweak in my back. Was briefly concerned his joviality was a false front and it was a trick to disable me via some pressure point. But he relaxed his grip and said, "I do have a sense of humour you know."

"I'll meet you at the boxing gym tomorrow. I've one more thing to sort out besides Benny's cronies."

"What?"

"I'm going to help Ronnie get back in training."

"Pissing in the wind," he said as he shook his head.

"We'll see."

I went outside and stood in the night air in the middle of Market Street and was just about to take a bite of my burger when Pitbull ran at me and shoved me over. My chips went flying everywhere and I landed hard on my arse on the blacktop. I wondered what was going on until I looked up and saw him grappling with Gareth Fitzrover who was armed with a hammer. His nose was bent right across his face.

Pitbull put him in an arm-lock and the hammer clattered to the concrete. Then he spun him around and knocked Fitzrover into a parked car with a three-punch combo. He finished with a suplex and Fitzrover was out cold on the bonnet of the car with his feet resting on the cracked windscreen. He put the hammer in the guy's inside pocket.

I was shaken up but thankfully still numb from the ale. Said, "I owe you one."

He straightened his suit jacket and replied, "No bother. You can buy me a drink. I fancy a nightclub. The night is young yet."

I projectile vomited. Must have been adrenalin and the thought that there were more people after my blood every day. Guess I wasn't as numb as I thought.

Pitbull shook his head and laughed. "If the cops come tell them this prick smashed the car up with the hammer." He jumped in a cab and disappeared into the night as I finally got back to my shaky feet.

I walked up towards Saint John the Baptist's church in a stupor. Fez, who'd been chatting in the kebab shop, was completely oblivious to the ruckus that had happened and I realised I was heading the wrong way and about-turned, staggering back down the street.

Fez shouted, "Meet me tomorrow."

I gave him a thumbs up and slid into the payphone booth next to the bus stop to tip off the cops about Fitzrover's hammer rampage and crossed over back to the office. The burnt-out shell of what was left of Victor's business put another layer of guilt in me and sobered me up. I thanked God for my friends. Things were coming to a head and I couldn't take any more messing around. It was time to get my rear in gear and strike back.

15

Woke up on the Sunday afternoon and shrugged off my hangover with a full body wash with cold water in the office sink. My nerves were jangly and I fought hard to keep my head clear. Headed out in the van up to the makeshift gym at the scout hut.

Fez was right at the back in the corner on his own in his red kimono. He had ten watermelons with what suspiciously looked like blown-up passport pictures of my face sellotaped to them. He proceeded to hack, slash and dice with his samurai sword and he looked like he was enjoying himself doing it. I waved and he gave me his trademark grin in return before training his attention back to the few fruits left unmauled.

Jack 'Chippy' Wall, the old boxing trainer, was helping his charges out with the pads. When there was a break in action he motioned me over. Climbed out of the ring and we sat down on the bench.

"Still working them hard I see, Chippy."

"Got some good prospects."

"I've got a better prospect."

"Send him up here, we've always got room."

"It's Ronnie Hag Fold Hurricane Finkell."

His face changed colour. "Fuck no."

"If I help him get clean, you whip him into shape."

"What part of *fuck no* don't you understand?"

"Come on, do me a favour."

"I don't owe you no fucking favours. Now you do me a favour and get to fuck with that man Finkell's name. I dedicated years to the bastard. No way in hell does he step foot in my gym. End of conversation."

"Can you at least point me in the direction of another

trainer?"

"The only person who'll go near him is Mickey Prender. I'm warning you all he cares about is the money, though. He'll pay him well, but he'll turn him into a fucking punch bag plum duff in six months."

"I think you're underestimating Ronnie."

"What did I tell you about not mentioning his name? He's like the Grey Lady: if you say his name he crawls out of the woodwork. Well, if he crawls in here he'll be back bouncing down that fire escape quicker than lightening. Here's Prender's number. Don't say I didn't warn you."

Fez was scaring me with the wild glee he was having chopping up the watermelons so I drove down to the Royal on Wigan Road and sat outside with a beer and a cigarette. Phoned Mickey Prender and told him Finkell's story.

He said, "It's all about narratives these days, Jacob. I'm wanting to sell fight tickets and the best way is a good story. You say he's already eight and zero, so we have a platform. He's known in your town. There's a heavy redemption kick. If Chippy Wall trained him he'll be well-schooled. I like it. How hooked on the drugs is he?"

"Very. But I reckon the thing behind it is that he doesn't see a life without boxing. He can't do nothing else so the addiction is his way of coping."

"I can feel a *but* coming."

Perceptive man. "The *but* is he needs to wean off the drugs. The NHS rehab places have a waiting list of six months and the private clinics will blow your budget."

"What are you suggesting?"

"I used to work in the hospital. I can do it. But that means shutting down my business. Which means loss of earnings."

"I'll give you five hundred a week for four weeks to help him clean up and take it back off his initial purses. He's got the rags to riches line and if he's as good as you say he is, we'll make it back no problem. What do you say?"

"I'd say it's a pleasure doing business with you."

Had another couple of pints, scoffed down a Cumberland sausage in a giant Yorkshire pudding from the landlady and tried my hardest not to think about Katy. Every time her scent and her voice played in my head I forced myself to think about the blue Fiesta and the attempted kidnapping. I needed the fire in my veins before I folded and ended up full-blown bat-shit insane with the relentless waves of guilt.

Drove back to the office around six and the door was unlocked. I tensed up and looked for a weapon in the burnt-out hairdressers but everything was ruined and covered in a thick acrid ash. Braced myself and sneaked up the stairs. Slowly pulled back the door with my heart in my throat. The blinds were drawn and there was no light on in the room. Saw a figure at the desk in the pitch darkness and charged at it.

16

I dived right onto the figure in the chair and we toppled over together. I put him in a chin-lock from behind and scissored my legs around his, stopping any wriggling.

"One of Benny's boys are you, dickhead? Talk now before I put you to sleep."

"Get the hell off me you crazy fool," came the strong Caribbean accented voice.

I let go straight away and helped old Victor back onto his feet.

"I didn't know it was you. Sorry, Mr Barnes."

"First you get my shop burned down, now you trying to strangle me. I'm not sure it was a good idea me helping you out."

"Why are you sat in the dark anyway?"

"It's my flat, I'll sit wherever the hell I want to. I was just using your office to work out my claim forms for the insurance. Can't use downstairs because it looks like a volcano been through there. Must have fallen asleep."

I opened the blinds to let some light in from Market Street and fixed us some drinks. As he was shuffling papers I had an idea. I reached into my box of stuff and took out a five mg benzo, slipping it into his beer before handing it over.

"Always the same with insurance," he said. "They're quick to take your money, but you have to be Spinoza to sort the paperwork to get them to pay out."

"Can I help?"

"I think you've done enough helping to last you a lifetime, gumshoe. Just give me that beer and keep quiet. Surely you can do that."

I made a pillow out of a pile of clothes, hunkered

73

down on the floor and thought through what was coming while Victor chugged the laced drink and shuffled the reams of documents. It took about an hour and a half until he entered dreamland. I waited until the snores rattled the walls and rolled his pants leg up and stole his gun. I couldn't ask to borrow it, prayed it wasn't registered and rationalised it was a better bet than buying one from some joker in town who might not be able to keep his mouth shut.

Took down the placard from the window that said *GIBFIELD PRIVATE INVESTIGATIONS* in huge red letters.

It hadn't been more than a week and I'd had a second career fly straight down the toilet. I figured I'd apply at the Tesco on Crab Tree Lane or do bar work or something from now on once the dust had settled.

Made sure Victor's breathing was fine and then I drove down Bolton Road looking for signs of life in Ronnie's flat but there were no lights and the curtains were wide open, meaning he wasn't twitching behind them. Carried on and turned left past Si's house, back past the gym and up on to Red Devil's.

He let me in with a broad grin, looking chirpy, smart and alert.

"What happened to you?" I said.

"Cleaning up, mate."

"Good for you." We shook hands and while he was looking sharp I chanced my luck. "Could I surf your couch for a week or two? Just while I sort some things out? I'll pay."

"No bother. A friend of our Ronnie's is always a friend of mine."

"Much appreciated." I meant it. I needed all the friends I could get.

Ronnie was shadowboxing in front of the TV, watching the Four Kings documentary on YouTube for the millionth time. My needling him had worked its magic but I knew the pull of the speed was still strong so we had to act fast. He was clearly still wired and I was under no illusion that as soon as the cravings kicked in when the shit started to leave his brain we'd be in for a hell of a struggle.

"Are you serious about being a fighter again?"

"Definitely."

"You feel ready?"

"Born that way."

"I've got you a potential promoter. Mickey Prender. Ever heard of him?"

"No. What about Chippy Wall?"

"He's not too happy with you."

"I bet Prince Naseem paid him to stop working with me."

Yep, he was still on the powder.

"Doesn't matter. If you want to box you can't do it with that shit rushing round your veins."

There came the stare. That intense, calculating, cold-blooded reptile glance. He didn't say anything.

I said, "You've done your rattle before in the hospital. You can do it again. We'll use the same sedatives."

He became a bundle of nervous energy, pacing around like a dervish. He said, "Red, we're going to need to rig your spare room up."

"What do you mean rig it up?" Red said.

"You're going to have to block up the window and reinforce the door. When Mr Whizz comes knocking, he doesn't fuck around."

I smiled at Red, who looked concerned for his flat, and then at Ronnie.

"Thanks, Jacob."

"That's what friends are for."

He nodded and knocked out a flashy combination.

"Here's what we need," I told them. "Plywood, screws and some two-by-fours for the door."

Red said, "What the fuck are you going to do to my flat?"

Ronnie laughed. I carried on. "Fifty quid's worth of quality powder to wean you off in increments. Bottles of water, and some foodstuffs. I'll leave that to you two. I'm going to bed down for the night. It's been a long week and I need some sleep."

I shut off all the lights, turned down the volume on the TV, got comfy as I could on the couch and was sound asleep not more than ten minutes after they'd left.

17

It must have been a deep sleep because I hadn't heard them come in or working through the night. I realised it was morning as Ronnie was sawing away at the pilfered wood in the sunlight streaming through the window and there was a healthy stock of grub in carrier bags on the floor. Red cooked us up a full English and we sat down to munch.

Over breakfast I phoned up the *Atherton Telegraph, Leigh Reporter* and the *Journal* on Red Devil's pay-as-you-go. Went like this:

Me: Good morning. I want to publish an obituary for tomorrow's paper.

Telegraph lady: No problem. What would you like it to say?

Me: I'd like it to read *Benny can burn in the fires of hell. Regards, the Chippy Wall Crew. In particular JGCF who was closer than most to the man.*

Telegraph lady: I'm sorry. Burn in hell? Are you sure that's an appropriate sentiment? It doesn't really sound right.

Me: It's a macho gang thing, you know what I mean? His friends will love it.

Telegraph lady: If you say so. It's your money.

Me: And it'll be in tomorrow?

Telegraph lady: In the evening edition.

Me: Thank you for your help.

My phone had been on charge and finally it came back to life. When I took a good look I felt a laceration in my soul when I checked the call listings. Katy's missed calls hit me like a sledgehammer and I pushed the food aside. It was the first time I'd actually faced up to acknowledging they were there in black and white and I just deleted them off. I needed no artificial reminders.

I phoned Fez and told him the ad was soon to be in place.

"They're going to be in for the shock of their lives," he said. I thought I could feel the shark's grin through the wires.

Detoxing off street drugs was never an exact science. The differences in purity, what they were cut with and different metabolisms made it difficult to time the stages. The good news with uppers like speed was that after the initial stage there'd be plenty of rest. The bad news was the psychological cravings, especially for Finkell.

I thought at first the chance of reinvigorating his boxing career almost had them beat and the first night wasn't too bad. Me and Red Devil took turns going for walks to stretch our legs in between keeping Ronnie company through the square we'd cut into the reinforced door. It was important he had human contact so as not go into sensory deprivation and also we had him write a full-signed statement that it was being done with his co-operation so he couldn't accuse us of kidnapping.

The second day was when the jovial joking about started, because he was working through the last few portions of his rations. By evening when he knew he was now going cold-turkey he started with the old, "Are you sure that's the lot? I think I should be due a bit more."

"You've chemically readjusted just fine, Ronnie. The rest is all psychological from here on in."

Fez was staking out Car Bank Street from Si 'Hairband' Braggins' roof. Without his knowledge. We didn't want to freak Si out so we figured it was best we didn't tell him, but we might also need a witness to rely on if our plan fell through and there was a full-blown shootout or something in the street. We both thought the balaclava boys might wait a few days rather come rampaging down and we were right as the first four nights were quiet. On Car Bank Street anyway.

Back in the flat, for the next two days with Ronnie, it was anything but.

First night was begging and pleading. I gave him small amounts of benzos in another reducing regime to take the edge off and even the odd neuroleptic to help him sleep. He ate ravenously and stayed well hydrated which was a good sign.

The third night the Red Devil and I had this to contend with:

Ronnie: You two are fucking dead if you don't let me go and get some. Dead. You hear me. Fucking dead, dickheads.

Us: Carry on threatening us and we'll get your nan down to wallop you.

Ronnie: I'm not scared of Jean Claude Gran Damme.

Us: Seriously?

Ronnie: OK don't tell her. She'll wallop me.

Us: Calm down then. You want to box you have to get clean.

Ronnie: I don't want to box. Fuck boxing. I'll tell the police you've kidnapped me.

Us: You signed the statement. I knew you'd pull that trick. Why would we kidnap you? Who would pay the ransom?

Ronnie: Don't take the piss. I need some.

Us: It's out of your bloodstream mate. Your mind will catch up very soon and you'll sleep like a baby.

Ronnie: You're both evil fuckers, and you're fucking dead.

Us: Do you want to earn money by winning fights and get your self-esteem back?

Ronnie: No. I want whizz.

Us: Are you telling me you want a dead cat for a belt instead of a Lonsdale belt?

Ronnie: I suppose not.

This routine went in cycles for the next two days. By the third day he looked back to his old self to the point we allowed him to come out of the makeshift detox room. His appetite was back, his skin had cleared up and his eyes were bright and relaxed.

I kept checking in with Fez on his nightshift surveillance and the next night we'd decided to up the ante and get in position.

During that day we let Ronnie walk around the block with us, close in on either side in case he made a run for a dealer's, but he was fine. He even broke into sprints to joke around with us from time to time. I reckoned he needed some responsibility to go with his returning chemical freedom and roped both him and Red Devil into turning the watch for the balaclava boys up a notch because me and Fez both knew it wouldn't be long now. And we were right. Because it happened that very same night.

18

The plan was simple. This is how it played out:

We had Dean Robinson in his van with the lights off half way up the street towards Derby Street. Fez was on Si's roof. Red devil was at the junction outside the post office and Finkell was at the junction near Bolton Road.

We thought this night could well be a dry run but we were bang on the money.

The blue Fiesta rolled around the corner and Finkell called it in, buzzing my phone. I signalled to Fez who dropped into Si's garden and hid in the privets. Dean swung his van and blocked off the road at the far end.

I was stood in the road as the bait and was supposed to fire a torch beam to freak the driver. I didn't. I was still sore at the attempted kidnapping so I'd rigged up Victor's gun with a makeshift silencer. We don't fuck around in this country either. I fired two bullets at the windscreen as Fez slid out his retractable stingers to bust the tyres. The shots sounded like pop bottles being run over as the silencer worked its magic.

The car careened to a halt, skidding down the road.

At the sound of the bust tyres the Red Devil drove my van into the road, climbed out and opened the back doors of the van.

Simon opened his front door, dressed in an electric yellow mankini, ripped his gas mask off with his arms full of freshly melted candle wax and shook his head. I heard him shout, "Absolute dickheads," in stunned shock as he recognised us, watching on in disbelief. We hit lucky as he was the only resident to come out at the noise.

Fez and I dragged them out one by one at gunpoint and had their arms zip-tied behind their backs in about twenty seconds flat. We scragged them into my van. Ronnie sloshed the Fiesta with petrol, set it on fire to distract the emergency services and ran, taking the long route back with Red Devil to our meeting place under the bridge at Hag Fold train station to avoid both witnesses and any drug dealers in case Ronnie got tempted to break his detox.

Dean had the all-clear as the traffic was non-existent and he screeched off into the night. Fez jumped in the driver's seat, I jumped in the passenger seat and we fucked off with our quarry.

19

Fez cruised carefully through the night streets. Said, "What the fuck are you doing firing a gun? We were supposed to be stealthy."

"These fuckers almost had me in the boot of their car."

"The idea was the car should look like joyriders blowing their tyres and running away. There'll be bullet casings at the scene, dickhead."

I hadn't thought of that. "Can't see the cops investigating that closely."

"Let's hope not."

We parked up under the bridge and switched up our captives into a black jeep with heavily tinted windows. The balaclava boys never said a word. I left the keys in my van for Ronnie and Red Devil to drive back to his place so as to have an alibi for the night.

We drove right to the top end of Hag Fold and parked up as deep into the woodland area known as The Rucks as the jeep would go. With the denseness of the trees we were pretty sure we had a couple of hours while it was dark.

I poked and prodded the last of the crew with Victor's gun as Fez directed them with his service pistol on a long march through the muddy undergrowth. We must have been going for about ten minutes when we stopped at what looked like a huge bundle of thickets. Fez swept the branches away and opened a steel door.

I said, "What the fuck is this?"

"An old bomb shelter. I use it to meditate sometimes."

"I've never seen this place before."

"Nobody else has been in it since World War Two."

We went underground into the bunker with our three guests. It was bigger than it appeared from up top; about fifteen feet by ten. Fez lit a couple of lamps and when the light kicked in we could all see he had lined the gaff from floor to ceiling in plastic.

The sight of the prepared killing room seemed to crack two of the three of my kidnappers as I could make out panicked breathing. The biggest one started giggling.

I was on the opposite side of the room and turned at the laughter. Pointed the gun at his head. Said, "Enjoy your chuckle while you still can. You won't be laughing for long."

"Fuck you."

I couldn't believe this prick. The attempted abduction flooded back into my head and I went a bit gun-giddy, pointing it at the guy's kneecap.

Fez said, "Control yourself."

"He's laughing in my face."

"We have a procedure, remember. I'm giving you an order to control yourself."

He must have seen the look on my face and went to grab the gun. It went off by accident just before he snatched it out of my hand.

20

"Forget it, Jacob, it's Atherton Town," Fez said, grinning to himself.

"What's so funny?"

"Your face. And my quip. Ring any bells, gumshoe? A certain film with Jack Nicholson. Nineteen seventy four."

"What the fuck are you on about?"

"You're telling me you've never seen Chinatown?"

I was still shook up from thinking I'd had a hand in another death. "Never fucking heard of it."

The sound of the gunshot had blasted around the bunker and I couldn't believe the bullet had missed. The two balaclava boys were swearing in shock and the third one who I thought I'd snuffed had definitely stopped giggling. The only one amused was Fez because he'd been the only one to recognise the round was a blank.

He said, "At least there's no bullet holes in the Fiesta."

He then dragged all three into the centre of the bunker. "Welcome to the pleasure dome gentlemen. Here's the deal. We're going to settle this the Atherton Town way. With a fair one-on-one straightener to sort this out once and for all. No holds barred but as soon as someone hits the deck, you back off until they get back up. Now who's first?"

The two who'd by now clearly cracked shook their heads and rolled to either side near the walls. The giggler said, "Let's fucking have it."

"Cut his hands free," Fez said to me. I shrugged and did as told.

Fez reached into his rucksack and pulled out his red kimono, took his top off and slipped the silk gown over his bare torso. The balaclava man shook his head, stretched his arms and cracked his knuckles.

I sat down to watch next to the other two who looked on in what I sensed was a mixture of trepidation and genuine curiosity.

At this point I could confabulate an epic fight scene. But the fight wasn't epic. It was strategic, savage, incisive, brutal, well-practised and over incredibly swiftly.

As far as I could make out, Fez went for the man's eye sockets, followed through with an elbow to the throat, hit him full force in the breastbone and before the guy had the chance to complete his fall backward Fez put his foot through his kneecap and splayed his leg. The guy never even had the chance to sling a slap.

Fez said, "Next," saw he had no takers and continued, "Now you three close your eyes and put your hands over your ears."

We all did as told but if I could hear the subsequent screaming, I'm convinced the other two could too. It did the trick. We had the information we wanted and we had full compliance while they let us hogtie them so they were immobile. For good measure I gave them a syringe full of crushed-up benzos each to add a bit of poetry to the situation. God only knows what they would have done to me had they driven me off the other day.

21

We blew out the lights, made sure we hadn't left anything behind bar our neo-fascists, and headed back through the undergrowth to Fez's jeep.

"What did you do to him to make him tell you their address?"

"I asked him nicely."

"Why did he scream then?"

"I was just helping him twist his leg back the right way while I was asking. He even offered me his keys, which was friendly of him."

Fair enough. "What's the address."

"A nice surprise."

It was a surprise all right. It was a church. Another one. A converted church on Tyldesley Road, annoyingly near Katy's home. It was once called Saint Anne's and been sold off to property developers who'd converted it into swanky apartments.

"I wonder which room is the confession booth," I said and immediately wished I hadn't, but he either never heard me or at least pretended so.

We both gloved up and slipped plastic bags on our shoes, held on with elastic bands. Inside, the décor was stunning but the place was a full-blown shithole. Bits of tin foil with what looked like the remnants of crack, burn marks in the carpets and some kind of shrine to their now deceased leader, Benny Big Bollock, alongside a cavalcade of other evil crackpots. Hitler and Mussolini stood next to each other in a picture blown up over the mantle-piece. Charles Manson, Dennis Nilsen and other murderers and serial killers were plastered all over the walls.

Fez said, "Here we go," and handed me a thick

bundle of papers. While he was raiding their fridge for food I flicked through. Terrorist manuals, urban guerrilla tactics, papers on withstanding interrogation, which may have explained why they were so quiet, and garbled predictions of an apparently coming apocalypse.

Topping it off was a list of assassination targets with detailed times, places and itineraries. Me and Fez were first on the list. Method of death: slow suffering. We were to be injected with drugs and tortured slowly. I realised how lucky I was. Dean happened to be driving by that day. God bless friendship was all that ran through my head. I ripped our names out as a shudder went through me.

We poked around a bit more and found the motherlode in a closet consisting of improvised explosive devices, plenty of uncut cocaine, other drugs I couldn't be sure of, a shotgun and a wedge of money that Fez and I stole and split down the middle.

"What a charming cadre of fellows," Fez said. "If only someone would have told them we won the war. The state of education these days, eh?"

I couldn't help but laugh at his grin. "I think we should go back, shoot the fuckers and bury them up The Rucks."

"If you think I'm getting mud on my lucky kimono from digging graves you just don't know me at all."

"What now then?" I said.

"We tip the cops off. Were you seriously suggesting we murder them in cold blood?"

"Don't look at me like that. They almost bloody had me in the boot."

"I think it's the Buddhists that say something like, 'revenge is like holding a hot brick. It only burns the palm of the holder'. Breathe deep and free yourself of the negativity by moving forward like water flowing down the Seven

Brooks."

"Are you taking the piss or is the church setting giving you flashbacks to the glow sticks?"

His mouth ticked a little at one corner but then he grinned again. "Let's go."

We went for a long drive to ensure we weren't being followed and then double-backed down Hindsford, past Shakerley, through Tyldesley and on into Astley. Used the payphone on Manchester Road across from my old Secondary School, Saint Mary's, to call the anti-terror hotline.

Sykes and I both studied psychology at the sixth form at that school and I did what every other fuckup like me does when they evaluate their circumstances: blame something or someone else. I figured that if the school had sent me to the Tesco on Crab Tree Lane after my A-Levels instead of encouraging me to go to university I'd never have stolen thousands of pounds worth of medication and things might have been just fine. I listened to my own thoughts and almost had myself convinced. Then out of nowhere I could have sworn I heard Liz Hurley's voice telling me I was being absolutely ridiculous and to get a grip. I swallowed my emergency neuroleptic and climbed back in Fez's jeep.

When we got back to Red Devil's after picking up kebabs for everyone there was screaming and shouting coming from the flat.

Fez led with his gun cocked after I'd used the fob to let him in and we rushed up the stairs and into the living room.

Ronnie was pissing himself and Red Devil was going ape-shit. I saw that Ronnie had locked him in the detox room.

"Now he knows what I felt like," Ronnie said.

22

Fez left later that morning as daylight broke. Must have been called back for a job somewhere but as usual couldn't tell us anything. He took my phone off me and put a sixteen-digit number into the contacts. Said, "Emergencies only. And I mean emergencies. Life and death stuff. Take it easy, lads. Good luck with the boxing, Ronnie." And he was gone.

As the morning news broke the rest of us sat round to watch.

On TV DS Mark Reed was talking to a reporter from the front of the police station.

He said, "We have arrested what appears to be an active terrorist cell who we believe highly dangerous with intentions to commit heinous acts of violence. However, while we appreciate, need and actively encourage the public's help with all forms of information in relation to serious crime, we cannot and do not support, want, nor condone any vigilante behaviour. Anyone with anything related to said incident is to telephone me directly on the following number…"

I thought the bust might boost Mark's career, but going by the look on his face he was preparing to cover for us if anyone had seen anything. Burning the car in front of Si's had given him the nod. In the car boot they'd found knives, ropes and drugs, intended for me and Fez.

I suspected he was definitely now on a shit-list somewhere. By that stage I was way beyond guilt. I was still wired and wiped out from adrenaline and rather than try and figure out a way to pay him back I thought it was best to keep my head down and just keep out of everyone's way in case I caused more bother.

Ronnie Finkell's training went like clockwork. A full

medical declared him fit and we focused on roadwork and light pads for the first few weeks. Given all the dodging debtors who he owed money to, he was in pretty good cardiovascular nick in the first place. I'd follow him in the van to shout encouragement and to keep him well away from any pushers.

By the third week I trusted him to go running on his own. At least that's what I told him.

Instead, I got Dean to drive me around and follow just in case, knowing Ronnie wouldn't recognise his vehicle.

I had the binoculars I stole from Fez's bag locked on Hurricane when I saw him break to a standstill and kind of crouch in the bushes at the end of Devonshire Road near the bridge. I scoped that he was looking at a middle-aged couple getting amorous in the summer heat and he dropped his shorts and looked like he was masturbating.

Dean said, "What's he doing?"

"You don't want to know."

From the top of the bridge, PC Colin Chase appeared in full uniform and slid down the sloped, flagged embankment. He strode up behind Ronnie, took a good look at him, flicked out his extendable stick and walloped him on the nut-sack. I made out, faintly, Colin say, "That's for selling me sherbet fucking dip, you cheeky cunt." Colin then climbed back up the embankment, jumped the railing and disappeared from view as Ronnie was bucking in the foetal position and letting out what sounded like '*yeeeeyeeeeeyeeee*' on the floor.

That hiccup aside, by the fourth week he'd insisted on full sparring and signed himself up for an eight-rounder. His blood was clean, he was in shape and he won all eight rounds, looking as sharp as the tip of one of his old syringes.

He took a fight once a fortnight throughout June and the first half of August and never even got hit. Granted his punch power looked like it needed some work but the hand speed, movement and natural flow of combinations dazzled everyone they put in front of him.

Mickey Prender did his bit with promotion and got the local press buzzing about his return from oblivion even though I sensed there were times Mickey wanted him to lose. He was a genuinely skilled fighter though, so there didn't seem to be any animosity.

Because of the press coverage there came ticket money. And in mid-August Mickey's darling, and the Northern Area flyweight champion, Ricky 'Big Bang' Blakey, wanted Ronnie's scalp – and the purse to go with it.

Ronnie was offered the mandatory defence with six weeks' notice and took it straight away.

Mickey said to me, "It'll be a nice send-off for Ronnie. Good few grand to set him up for retirement."

"How do you know he won't win?"

"Have you seen Blakey punch? Just keep the towel ready and be a friend when it gets messy."

It got me thinking. Was I overestimating the Hag Fold Hurricane because he was my friend, or were they all underestimating him?

He didn't care. Said, "I want the belt. If you throw a towel I'm disowning you as a friend. I'll go out on my shield."

Was he brave or stupid? That's what everyone was asking around town. Most people agreed it was a mixture of both. Whatever, he'd clawed back a hell of a lot of respect.

23

The fight was the first official outdoor boxing match in Atherton Town's history. The mid-September weather was unusually dry and it was the perfect temperature to get pulses racing in the crowd at Alder House, the ground of Atherton Collieries Football Club. It had been there since it was first established back in 1916 when the club was set up by miners to raise funds for folks involved in the war. Every blade of grass was tightly packed with chairs, and the tickets were sold out from the front row to the stands. I estimated about four thousand in attendance. Mickey had driven all of the sales and the entire roadshow.

Ronnie played the media like a pro. At the final head-to-head, when Ricky Blakey said, "I'll have your teeth, knobhead," Ronnie flipped out his dentures and replied, "You can take them now if you're so desperate for 'em." The clip went viral on social media and a new underdog, so beloved by the British public, was born.

The betting suggested he *was* an underdog. He was eight to one against just to last the distance. I told all the boys including Victor Barnes and even tipped off Father Kay anonymously to back the fight going twelve rounds so he could buy a new crucifix and stop whinging about the one stolen in 1991. Everyone from the old days in Atherton Town showed up on fight night. A lot of folks said they were coming just to watch him get knocked the fuck out.

In the dressing room he wanted to be left alone with his thoughts. I made sure all the water he drank was from our bottles and any food was pre-packaged. It wasn't that I distrusted Mickey; he never messed with the ring padding or pricked us about, but I knew he had a lot riding on the fight. His fighter was his meal ticket, and being twenty two he had a lot longer of a career in front of him than Ronnie. I headed to ringside early with my old friends the Brindle brothers on one side and the Grimshaw brothers on the other as my back up just in case of any shenanigans and I had Dean Robinson watching the bookmakers.

The undercard was eventful. I repaid Paul 'Pitbull' Horrocks for saving me from getting a hammer in my skull by getting Mickey to give him his pro boxing debut. He had the crowd on their feet in a barnstormer, winning by sensational knockout in the third.

I also gave Si 'Hairband' Braggins his debut. He too got the cheers going and was putting on good show until his opponent bottled it and bit him. It was clear as day but the ref didn't see it. Si didn't mess around at the best of times and had the biter in a Ju-Jitsu hold after roundhouse kicking him on the jaw and sending his gumshield flying into the audience. Pandemonium broke out and I had to send in the Brindles and the Grimshaws to get Si off him and back up the other cornermen. Took them nearly five minutes.

The main event was announced. Red Devil was in the front row trying to get an *Ooh Ahh Cantona* chant going. They played the National Anthem and everyone stood up and belted out God Save the Queen and the fighters came to the ring.

First up came Ricky 'Big Bang' Blakey to a happy hard-core dance tune that was called *Now is the Time* by DJ Scott Brown.

Next came Ronnie 'Hag Fold Hurricane' Finkell. He walked out to P Diddy's *Bad Boy For Life*. When the opening lyric mentioned *half man, half drugs* the crowd erupted into howls of laughter. They weren't laughing for long.

For the first four rounds Ronnie put on a masterclass. Switching up, reflexes honed from the paranoia years razor-like, the younger man couldn't get anywhere near him. He was pot shotting, in and out with flashy combinations, absolutely flying. Rounds mounted up.

Dean Robinson came back to me by the seventh. Said, "Bookies are laying off the tenth round. Big money."

I looked over at Mickey in the crowd, who was sweating heavily. He caught my eye and looked away.

It wasn't a fix. But they were picking their moment. I thought things were going too well. It didn't matter that we were now eight rounds in the bank if he was going to get annihilated in around five minutes.

At the end of the eighth Ronnie was focused but flagging. Those in the crowd who still had a vendetta, probably over being ripped off in the past, were starting to begrudgingly cheer his mastery of the ring. I went over to the corner.

He said, "I'm tired but it's an easy cruise now. Only four left."

"He's holding something back and he needs to stop you anyway. Switch on. Danger time."

Ricky flew out in the ninth like a tasered rhino and pinned Ronnie into the neutral corner. He managed to slip and slide but some ferocious body shots took the wind out of him. He fired back but no matter how many times he hit Ricky, the lad never even blinked. It had been like Joe Calzaghe schooling Jeff Lacy, minus any damage to Blakey's face whatsoever. Until now.

With twenty seconds left Ricky caught Ronnie with a left hook that staggered him hard and went back to the body. Half the crowd went up on their feet baying for blood and started to boo when Ricky went back behind his guard and appeared to miss with a right cross.

I could see they'd trained perfectly in the scenario, softening him up, shaking him up and then here they were coming.

As he sat down at the end of the ninth I said, "Listen mate, he's teeing you up. If you're hurt I'm stopping it."

"I am hurt. I'm not jacking, though. They can carry me out."

"Fancy some whizz?"

He looked at me like I'd told him he'd won the lottery. "What about piss testing?"

"I've got it all worked out."

I gave him a fresh bottle. "Mr Whizz doesn't fuck around does he?"

And that was it. He necked a pint and was up like Pop Eye after his spinach. He pranced around the ring in the tenth like someone overdosed on ecstasy at the Hacienda. At one stage he was even doing the dance from the track *Walk Like and Egyptian* by the Bangles. Ricky was feeling the pressure and clearly bamboozled by the speed of the recovery. He caught Ronnie flush with a one-two but he just shrugged it off and gave a huge gummy grin, flicking his gum shield in and out by waggling his tongue. He was bouncing around with his hands by his hips, not giving a fuck and loving every moment. Fired back but still hadn't left a mark. Even though they didn't hurt, every punch scored.

Ricky had both punched himself out and knew he'd thrown away his belt. He was too far behind even if he got knockdowns and Ronnie was just too elusive.

The fight was over in a flash and Ronnie got a standing ovation. The crowd were pissed up and doing the Egyptian dance from the front row to the back.

The fighters stood in the centre of the ring as the MC read out the lopsided scorecards and said, "We have a unanimous decision. Your winner, from Atherton, Greater Manchester, United Kingdom, and the new Northern area flyweight champion, Ronnie Finkell!" The ref raised his hand in the air as the DJ dropped ACDC's *You Shook Me All Night*

Long.

Ronnie motioned to me and I reluctantly climbed in the ring with him. As I did so I saw Mickey staring hard at us and jabbering his way into his mobile. I sensed trouble, but I kept it to myself. The Hag Fold Hurricane had put on a full-blown exhibition of the sweet science and he'd earned his night of glory. Flashbulbs from the sports photographers popped and journalists were on the ring apron shouting his name.

He whispered, "They're coming to do the drug test. What's the plan?"

"There was no whizz in the drink. It was sherbet dip mixed with baking soda."

"You scheming cunt," he said through a grin as he looked at the belt.

I pointed at it and replied, "Better than a dead cat, right?"

24

We partied hard and carried the newspapers round from pub to pub in town for the next forty eight hours. They shook Ronnie's hand and slapped him on the back. He even kept sensible on the drink, never mind any drugs. We had local photographer Darryl Kinney follow us round to document the celebrations.

Great times.

Memories I cling onto, to this day.

People were speculating Ronnie would go on to challenge for the British flyweight title but it never happened.

There were no more memories to make and no more pictures to take.

Because Ronnie 'Hag Fold Hurricane' Finkell was found dead four days later.

25

He was found lying on his back in the middle of the field near Saint Richard's primary school. Some sick ghouls had took his:

> Title belt
> Trouser belt
> Suit jacket
> Shirt
> Shoes
> Socks

And even took his false teeth, before the dog walker who later found him rang the police and an ambulance. They left his pants on, so at least he kept his dignity.

It was said that he died happy; with a smile on his face. Although no one knew for sure whether he was smiling or if the erstwhile tooth fairy had messed with his facial features as a piss-take.

There was nothing suspicious reported at the autopsy. No drugs. No assault. No underlying heart condition or any type of brain damage from the boxing. The only medical abnormality detected was a mild case of fucking rickets. It seemed the universe was playing tricks.

Cause of death was put down as sudden adult death syndrome. Hard Living. He was thirty six years old. I can't make sense of it to this day. The press sensationalised it and there were people asking about doing a documentary but I wanted nothing to do with it. It was the last straw.

***

His death sent Mickey Prender ballistic. He figured I'd deliberately sent Ronnie in as a ringer to take the zero from his best fighter and use his backing to leapfrog to a bigger promoter. As was obvious I did no such thing. Helping a friend is all I was doing. He'd lost two potentially lucrative careers in one week. And he sent some of his cronies to extract his money back. From me.

They came when I was giving Victor Barnes his gun back at the entrance to the barber shop, which was being refurbished. Victor was about to tear me a new arsehole when he stopped shouting and said, "I think you might need it. There's a group of fellas heading your way and they don't look too happy."

"There's no bullets in it. They're blanks. What am I going to do? Deafen them into submission?"

"Did you seriously think I had a loaded gun? Do I look like a complete moron?"

There were about seven or eight coming from both directions. There was nowhere to run.

I took my phone out and dialled the sixteen-digit number Fez had left in my contacts. The most incredible thing happened.

On the screen a text came up. It said:

You've got more friends than you think

The whole of Market Street started filling up with cars and vans and even a lorry came by with a huge Union Jack on it. They kept driving round and round at high speed, turning down the side streets and circling back again. Over fifty vehicles. Motorcycles rocketed up on the pavements. One van pulled up on the kerb outside the post office. The door slid open and they blasted out the tune of *Self Preservation Society* which blended into *Rule Britannia* and finally Elgar's *Pomp and Circumstance*.

Mickey Prender and his boys all froze, as shocked as

I was.

Then all the cars slammed on and the doors opened and the motorbikes roared up and braked. I heard what sounded like a hundred guns cocking and being pointed right at them as the music hit its crescendo.

A bloke on the bike flicked up his visor.

Looked Mickey and his crew up and down and said, "I suggest you lot fuck off. Very quickly."

They did.

Once they were gone the traffic dispersed and just melted away.

I turned to Victor who looked as stunned as I was.

Said, "Did you just see what I just saw?"

He just nodded, wide-eyed.

"God bless the British Armed Forces."

26

Ronnie Finkell's funeral took place two weeks after he'd been found dead. It was a warm and bright morning at the back end of September and the sun beamed down on Atherton cemetery on Leigh road. Great oak trees lent some shade but the casket gleamed and glistened. Conker shells were scattered along the little concrete footpaths between the headstones as the boys and I walked through to where Father Percival Kay was to conduct the burial.

The ceremony itself had been a pretty upbeat affair. Red Devil impressed everyone with his eloquence when he read a eulogy, even managing to mention Eric Cantona in some sporting analogy I couldn't really understand. I didn't get up to speak, being too numb and also full of trepidation.

I was trying to work out the best time to admit to the priest that it was me who was responsible for Mr P Ricketts thinking his confession had been leaked and not him. He looked more haggard and ragged than I'd ever seen him.

I knew how false accusations ate people up from the inside, like with me and the crucifix that I could have sworn I saw through Sykes' window when we picked him up on the way. Not to mention being arrested for Katy's murder.

The thing was I knew I needed him to know it was me with the bug. There was no way I could let him carry the burden of the murder-suicide. But I didn't trust his tempter if we were alone so I figured it would be best to whisper it to him while people were throwing roses and dirt after the coffin had been lowered into the grave. He'd have to keep his composure for the sake of the dignity of the occasion.

I'd already texted Dean Robinson to be waiting outside on Liscard Street in his van so I could make a sharp exit after my confession. I texted him again to make doubly sure:

11:00 sharp plz b there

We'd had half an hour to kill after the funeral, so Fez, Mark, Colin, Sykes, Braggins and I took the scenic route from Mayfield Street through Atherton Park on the way to the cemetery. Brightly coloured flowers that the local community group had planted were in full bloom all around. We'd all played football, drank lager and cider and partied through our teenage years in that place back in the day and we were all strangely quiet. I suspect like most folks at a funeral we were not only praying for the deceased but were actively reminded of our own mortality and the snap of the fingers that seems to be the zip of time. Decades of memories flashing through our minds in blinks. I had a much more important thing to worry about than mortality, and that was Father Kay.

Colin broke the silence. "Sad innit."

Fez said, "We are not here to get all maudlin. We're celebrating his life, not mourning his death."

The lads were surprised. I said, "Don't be shocked boys, Chris had an enlightening experience in the confession booth." Couldn't resist it.

Everyone burst out laughing. Apart from Fez who fixed me with the look as his knuckles cracked when he instinctively balled his hands into fists.

I reflexively took two steps back and hid behind Si. "Just a joke."

Luckily we were coming out of the park and heading down Leigh Road as the funeral cars passed in convoy carrying fellow mourners which put Fez off causing a scene.

We joined the folks by Ronnie's grave. Huge assemblages of flowers were laid out in the shape of boxing gloves, red ones and golden ones. There was a big crowd and they made way for us to get in close.

Father Percival Kay did his speech, and I was surprised by both his melancholy and his genuine sincerity in his duties. After he'd finished and people started to come forward to leave trinkets and scatter flowers in the hole I took a deep breath and ambled over.

He tried to pretend he hadn't seen me even though I saw his jaw clench when I stood next to him.

I quickly checked my phone. Dean had sent me a thumbs-up emoji. I took a deep breath and said, "Father, I have a confession to make."

"Now isn't the time for messing around, Gibfield."

"I'm serious. You know the *erm*, well, the murder-suicide thing? Well, it was me who told his wife he was having the affair. I can prove it wasn't you who leaked his confession."

His brow furrowed and pupils dilated and I think I could make out grinding teeth. "Go on."

"Well, it was me."

He spoke very slowly. "And how, pray tell, is that possible, Jacob."

I inhaled again, deeply. "I bugged the confession booth and gave his wife the recording for five hundred pounds. I still have a copy of the recording so you know I'm telling the truth. I also confess I'm a thief and a liar."

Father Kay stuck out his bottom lip and nodded. I let out my breath. I couldn't believe how well he was taking it.

That's the thing when you're being strangled; you don't quite realise it's happening until a couple of seconds later. It was only when he bellowed, "You bugged the fucking confession booth. I'll kill you!" that my brain caught up with the scuffle.

He had both hands round my throat and I couldn't buck him off. We stumbled back and tripped over the mound of mud and fell into the grave onto the top of Ronnie's coffin, rolling around as I tried to wrestle his grip from me but I couldn't get free.

"The fucking confession booth? You fucking little prick!"

I heard some *ooohs* and an *oh my word* in a cacophony of shock from those at the graveside while Colin and Mark used their police techniques to pin his arms round his back.

I scrambled out of the freshly dug earth and made a sprint for it. As I was running Ronnie's mother thrust a letter in my hand and all I could hear was Sykes, Braggins and Fez laughing hysterically as I dashed toward the small gate that led to Liscard Street.

Fez shouted, "Told you. Desecrating graves."

I shouted back, "Watch out for those glow stick angels, bellend."

He stopped laughing and scrambled after me.

I jumped in Dean's van. He gave me the once over because I was covered in mud. I pointed to Fez gaining on me and my voice was in a panic. All I could manage was:

"Go."

27

As Dean whisked me away from the cemetery I opened the letter from Ronnie's mother. It said:

Thank you, Jacob. I know Ronnie was a pain in the backside to put it mildly, but of course everybody is heartbroken that he's no longer with us. I just wanted you to know that the last few weeks have been the happiest I've seen him in his life.

When he saw his picture in the paper with the title belt slung across his shoulder he signed it and wrote "Dedicated to my old mate Jacob Gibfield" in the centre of the page and framed it. I hope you don't mind if I keep it on my wall. You helped to give him his life back, as short as it ended up being, so once again thank you. Take care,
Sincerely,
Winifred Finkell.

I thought I'd seen it all in my time working at the psychiatric hospital, and I had a stack of *thank you* letters that brought the odd tear to my eye on the odd occasion I flicked through them. But I'm not ashamed to say that the floodgates opened and dripped on the letter, smearing the ink; for Ronnie, for Katy and for all the rest of the crazy shit us humans have to put up with.

Slipped the letter in my funeral suit pocket and told Dean to take a detour for one last look at Ronnie's flat.

We pulled up on Bolton Road and I was surprised to find bunches of flowers on the landing of the stairwell from his neighbours which made me blubber that bit more. I was more surprised to find the door unlocked and yet everything was untouched so far as I could make out.

I pulled up a rickety chair from the kitchen and sat down next to the giant gnome with the joint in its mouth.

The quietness of the place made it finally sink in that he was no longer with us. I rested my elbow on the gnome's head and leaned back. The chair collapsed on itself and the gnome tippled over and its head fell off.

Inside I saw a wad of notes and some other paper. Reached in and took out a cheque stub for a thousand pounds and a note. I read it three times just to make sure:

Thank you for confirming it was Gibfield and Ferry that fucked our Benny's head up. Here's your pay. Nice doing business with you Hurricane.

So there it was. That's how they knew it was us in the first place. I did wonder how Ronnie kept up his drug habit after I'd been busted with the pharmaceutical racket. After all he always consumed more than he'd ever made knocking it out.

The backstabbing motherfucker sold us out for a measly grand to keep himself in amphetamines. The tears dried up and a large part of me was glad the traitorous, scheming little cunt was dead.

I sat there nodding my head, my body shaking with rage. I took some deep breaths and reasoned that was the drugs warping his personality and deep down he was just another victim of addiction. I had to, otherwise I could see myself digging the bastard back up.

I threw the gnome's head at the wall and collected the few hundred stashed quid and felt a tiny bit better.

Jumped back in Dean's van and asked him to drive me to out of Atherton Town. I needed to get the hell away from the place.

"Where to?" Dean said.

I didn't know. So at random said, "Hit Wigan Road. The road to Wigan Pier."

Why not? Maybe I'd stand on the Pier and survey my future. If it was a good enough place for George Orwell to contemplate life, I figured it was good enough for me.

For the first few miles I didn't say a word. It was when we passed the skate ramps at Ince Park and got flashbacks of decades ago summers riding the old half pipe with Ronnie and the other lads I just cracked up into hysterics. The kind of laughter that just comes out of its own volition when things in your life are just fucked up and that's all you can do.

Dean kept looking over and seemed somewhat worried I'd finally gone insane. I told him about Ronnie stitching us up and he laughed all the way to Wigan town centre. I gave him a couple of grand from the money I'd won betting on Ronnie going the distance as a thank you and he let me out and blasted a couple of beeps as he u-turned and headed home.

28

I wandered around aimlessly until the feeling hit me that Wigan wasn't far enough away. Found myself staring through the travel agent's window. Spied my reflection in the glass and could visibly see Father Kay's finger marks around my neck.

I swapped the idea of a quick flight for a coach to Catalonia, departing the next day, so I could viscerally feel the growing distance. Paid in cash at the travel desk and took the location tracker off my phone so nobody could follow me.

I traversed England, passing city after city all the way down to the coast of the United Kingdom to Dover. Boarded the ferry to France and waved goodbye to those famous White Cliffs.

Carried on through the Calais rurality and into the evening and night passing through the beautiful city of Lyon, sleeping on and off.

I finally woke sometime in the early morning just as the coach passed the stadium of the Catalan Dragons and then on and over the Pyrenees mountains.

Down the windy, dusty roads and eventually reaching my destination of the tranquil little resort of Malgrat De Mar on the Costa Brava. I booked a tour of the city of Barcelona for during the week and checked out the taxi fares to Lloret if I fancied some nightclubs later on when my nerves had settled.

I took my case from the coach, breathed in the Spanish air and saw my hotel was perfectly placed just over the road from a beautiful sandy beach.

I shaved and showered the journey away, got some lunch and slept by the pool in the Mediterranean sun after strolling barefoot in the sea.

I was jobless, homeless, single, approaching forty and at least partly responsible for quite a bit of chaos. One friend was dead, what could have been my soulmate had been murdered, my other friends' careers clearly jeopardised and it was a safe bet I could count myself excommunicated from my church. I looked out at the rolling sea and the horizon and saw the raw beauty in the stillness and as it met the sky it occurred to me to me to hope beyond hope that maybe, just maybe, the deeds of us humans really aren't that significant in the grand scheme of things after all. I willed myself to just relax.

As evening came I changed into some chinos and a crisp cotton shirt and sank some beers as the sky turned purple and red. I got a text on my phone from Si Braggins.

It said, *Mark got demoted. He's back with Colin in uniform. You know what that means. Check this and cheer up.*

There was a link to a video. I clicked on it and pressed play:

Mark was on stage looking coked out if his eyeballs. It was in the big function room above The Mill bar. Stand-up comedy night.
Mark snatched the microphone from the stand and said, "I've secretly been writing poetry for a long time and this is my debut reading it to anyone else (smattering of applause). My ambition is to one day follow in the footsteps of the world-renowned poet, who spent some of his life in this very town, the great Mr Lemn Sissay."
(The crowd clapped and cheered Lemn Sissay's name)
"But for the purposes of tonight, my poem, titled Ode To Atherton Town *is owed the inspiration from another poet from the Northwest, a certain John Cooper Clarke.*
(More cheering).
Some will this say this is a pastiche of one of his most famous poems, but I describe it as a major homage, both to him and to our home town."

(crowd expectant)

It was a good intro and he had the crowd in the palm of his hand.

Until this:

Mark said, "Ready? Here we go.
The Seven Brooks are full of rats
The fucking slags are fucking fat
The wind is fucking nippy
And No one beats our chippies
Cos everybody's Happy in Atherton Town"
(Half the crowd broke into laughter but the other half looked distinctly uncomfortable. A group of women walked out after one of them threw a glass that smashed on the stage. Paul 'Pitbull' Horrocks and Si 'Hairband' Braggins were looking nervous doing security at the edge of the seats. Mark didn't even look up from his sheet of paper and rattled through the following verses:
"The fucking football's fucking streaky
fucking streaker's fucking geeky
The drug dealer's fucking cheeky
And the clock is fucking creaky
But everybody's happy in Atherton Town

The amphetamines are weak
The fucking pimps are fucking sleek
The price of charlie's through the roof
Your blood is 100 percent proof
Cos everybody's happy in Atherton town
(The half of the crowd with him were on their feet and whooping, joining in with the last line of every verse but the other half were getting more and more outraged. Si had some heckler in a headlock and Pitbull had another one in an arm lock. Mark snorted some more cocaine off his

thumbnail then carried on)
The fucking roads are fucking packed
Even your gran is hooked on crack
(That was the line that did it. People started shouting, 'How fucking dare you, this is a respectable town, you cheeky bastard,' and things of that nature that were hard to pick up from the audio. More glasses flew. Si and Pitbull were getting overwhelmed, struggling to control the sheer numbers trying to get near the stage)
Even the cops are fucking told
Not to walk through our Hag Fold
But everybody's happy in Atherton Town

The fucking job centre is shut
The Undertaker can't believe his luck
Every Sat'day night there is a ruck
And none of us could give a fuck
Cos everybody's Happy
In Atherton Town"
He paced around the stage basking in the cheering from half the crowd and ignoring the other half baying for his blood. Uniformed police arrived, wading in with Si and Pitbull. Chairs were flying everywhere. Mark shouted, "Thank you! How do you know you're over Atherton in a helicopter? Dangle your legs out of the door and see if your shoes go missing!"

At that point the crowd flipped even more and almost breached the stage. The cops escorted Mark out of the building and the video ended.

By nightfall I'd just about stopped laughing and could barely keep my eyes open. As I walked past the lobby to the lift, I could have sworn I heard a faint humming of a helicopter through the doors that led out onto the street. I rubbed my face and figured it was just my ears being used to the thrum of the motorways.

I stuck Liz Hurley on the wall above the bed, closed the curtains of my balcony and nudged the screen door open a crack for the sweet breeze to keep me cool. Got undressed and slipped under the fresh, soft sheets without a care or worry in the world, drifting into a deep, dreamless sleep.

It must have been the beer that gave me the urge to piss and I sat upright. I felt cold steel pressing into my forehead. In a millisecond I tried to blink my vision back and orient to the room. I could only make out a black shape in front of me.

"Say your prayers, motherfucker," followed by the cocking of a pistol.

I pissed and shit the bed there and then.

I saw the figure pull off the mask and made out the pearly-white shark grin beaming luminous in the dark.

He threw my phone down on the bed. It blasted out *I Saw An Angel* by DJ Hixxy at full volume.

Fez said, "Now we're even. You should see your face."

Then he disappeared onto the balcony and dived off.

I flipped on the light, rechecked my pulse to make sure I wasn't having a heart attack and ripped the soiled sheets off the bed as the music boomed.

The thrust of helicopter rotor blades billowed the curtains. I waved my fist at the arsehole but had to admit he'd got me good and proper.

As I ran the shower I spied in the reflection of the pane, in the mirror behind me, the bug sellotaped to my lower back alongside upon inspection what turned out to be a neuroleptic tablet. The sneaky prick.

I knew there and then I'd go home one day.

You could take the lads out of proud, old Atherton Town but you couldn't take Atherton Town out of the lads.

We could never leave the fucking place forever.

Something would always bring us back.

Epilogue

Getting away for a while was wonderful but I missed home and Christmas was approaching. There was nowhere else on Earth I'd ever want to celebrate it. The fact I was running out of dosh may well have been a fair factor also. You could only live like a cocaine-fuelled rock star on a bus driver's budget for so long.

Was winging my way back to Manchester airport and was overwhelmed with memories of a Christmas Eve from a few years earlier, not long before I got caught with those boxes of tablets sellotaped to my torso…

I thought she was trying to kiss me. Some mistletoe trick. Tilted my head away from hers and put my hand up between us.

She hadn't been in long and had eyed me with something bordering on outright hostility in brief exchanges the previous day, so I was surprised at how quickly the Christmas spirit had worked its magic.

Obviously inappropriate relations between staff and patients were a no-no and as such I was trying to delicately disentangle us while trying to see the funny side. Happened to look at a group of other patients sat on the little bench watching the episode unfold and thought they'd be amused. Instead I saw their expressions were ones or either horror or incredulity. Slightly odd. As was the tightening grip. Around my neck. I reluctantly faced what I thought was my amorous acquaintance, instinctively leaned back to keep out of distance of puckered lips and chanced a glance. Teeth bared, raw hatred beaming from the screwed-up eyes. This wasn't kissing. She was trying to kill me.

This entire experience happened in slow motion in under five seconds. Prised her fingers from my throat as assistance came quickly from colleagues who had rounded the corner at my voice saying something like, "Please desist from assaulting staff." What I wanted to shout was,

"Stop strangling me, you whopper," but you've got to keep professional, even while someone is attempting to murder you.

"He keeps calling me names, the bastard," she said.

"Eh? I've not even met you proper yet, why would I call you names?" I said.

"Don't take the piss, I've heard you all day."

Derogatory hallucinations. Torturous affliction. In this instance, attributed to me.

I tried, *"I think we've got off on the wrong foot. I'm here to help you."*

"Don't come that game with me, I'll give you what for, you swine. I'll swing for you."

The other staff led her to the clinic while she bellowed threats and expletives.

The nurse in charge smiled as she said, *"You're a charmer aren't you?"*

"Fuck off. I'm just glad she didn't have mistletoe after all. Talk about a femme fatale."

She laughed. *"Get a brew and a mince pie."*

Staffroom: strong tea and a bit of buffet food. One bite was all I managed before the bells rang out. Neither sleigh bells nor Christmas bells. Instead: the alarm bells.

The infirmary, the unit, Roy Wood from Wizzard blaring out the radio at full blast. Christmas bloody Eve.

Ran down the corridor to the electronic panel that indicated the ward below. Sprinted through the unit, bleeped myself out and clattered down the stairs, thinking please nobody hanging, nobody dead or dying or beaten to a pulp. When you're prepared for the worst then anything less is a relief.

Doors wide open, a bank staff says, "Seclusion room."
"Ta."
The back end of a scuffle.
Someone says, "Take his arm off me."

We lay him down on his front on the padded bed. Well drilled staff extraction, dragging out the person in front of us backwards as we hastily exited the seclusion room, slammed shut the door and bolted it locked. The fella inside the room leapt up, going apeshit and kicking Holy Hell at the door from the inside. Me and the others, outside, catching our breath.

"You'd not make a sprinter," the nursing assistant said with a grin.

"Six seconds it took me, you cheeky bastard. I counted."

He laughed, wiped sweat off his forehead then came over all weary. Said, "What a flipping cock up this is."

"Go on."

"Well to cut a long story short, this fella," he said, indicating with his thumb to the bloke knocking seven bells out of the woodwork, "thought his missus was cheating on him, having affairs like. She said he's going bonkers, can't convince him it's in his head. Gets the GP involved, who gets the consultant psychiatrist who assesses him as delusional and brings him in here.

Been with us three months. We've worked with him, talked with him, tried him on numerous tablets, nothing working. He's getting in a bad state, not eating properly and all the rest of it.

Anyway, the consultant decides we need some drastic action so he prescribes emergency ECT. Thinking hopefully we get a rapid response and he can have some Christmas dinner with his wife. So we give him something to keep him calm for the treatment and walk him up to the suite.

In the meantime one of our staff has gone for a run round the flash on his break. You know the flash is a dogging hotspot. Well, he goes for a piss in the bushes and who does he see on a Christmas dogging sesh in the woods? Only this chap's missus. Apparently she's a regular. She's just admitted on the blower. She had to, she'd been seen in action."

"Bollocks."

"Swear down. Our staff phones the ward to tell us, but obviously nobody is in the office. Meanwhile yon mon is having his

frontal lobes zapped. Staff gets back, frantically explaining, we run up to ECT but it's too late by then. Our patient is sat there chewing on dry toast."

"Oh my God."

"We bring him back down to the ward, and tactfully inform him of the situation. Needless to say, he went absolutely fucking ballistic." He puffed his cheeks out and shook his head. *"Can you watch him for five minutes while I nip for a quick fag."*

"Aye," I said. That's all I could manage. Aye.

It was important when secluding someone to ensure they could see a clock and another human through the reinforced glass panels so as not to go into sensory deprivation. Also you had to watch in case they fashioned a makeshift ligature from clothing, so I pulled up a chair and took a seat.

He came straight over and shouted, "Who are you?"

"I'm from upstairs, I'm just covering for a while."

"Well these fucking crackpots have kidnapped me, drugged me up and run electric through my brain. Have you ever heard owt like it? I fucking told them she was messing about, I told them. Look what they've done! Telling me I'm delusional for months? They're delusional. I'll rip their fucking heads off," he shouted.

I nodded empathetically. What could you say to that? I said, "Shocking."

"Shocking? Are you a fucking comedian sunshine?"

I hadn't said it to take the piss, I was genuinely shocked at the situation. I felt a right dickhead but fair play to the bloke because he started to laugh which diffused the tension a fair bit.

Slade. Merry Christmas Everybody on the radio. Me, thinking: what the fuck is going on.

The Infirmary, the unit, Christmas bloody Eve.

Staff came to take over and another one let me out. We did the merry Christmases and the like and I went outside for a smoke myself.

Snow turning to slush.

Bewildered.

The consultant was sucking on a cig and pacing up and down under the canopy. From cocksure to a shivering wreck in three hours.

"These things happen, Doc," I said.

"You think so?"

"It's a funny old profession, psychiatry."

"Yes, I suppose it is."

He didn't seem reassured and I couldn't have given two fucks whether he was or not in all honesty. Saved by the emergency bleep. It was a little black pager type of thing then and the voice came over to instruct me to go to a ward the next shelter down. Dementia and Alzheimer's and other degenerative neurological conditions.

Flicked my cig and kicked up snow. Through the main doors, thinking please nobody hanging, nobody dead or dying or beaten to a bloody pulp. Very different environment from the acute, this. It needed folks with the patience of Saints and not a sinner amongst them, and that's what they had.

Commotion at the top of the ward. A big bear of a bloke with a nursing assistant in a headlock. Was saying, "I've tow'd thee to keep the hell out of my road."

They were trying to change his trousers for clean ones and he was confused and disoriented, lashing out. Non-threatening body language, non-confrontational verbals, continual reassurances muttered every twenty seconds and they got him sorted. Clean clothes, fed, cared for. A very different type of work from the acute. Staff with the patience of Saints.

We swapped Merry Christmases and cliched jokes along the lines of, "Never mind three wise men, can't seem to find one in this office," and the odd flirt saying, "You playing Father Christmas, gracing us with your presence? You can empty your sack for me tonight if you want." Banter and gallows humour flowed as fast as the non-alcoholic wine. I said I'd let myself out and as I neared the exit I heard a nurse crying in the toilets.

Back on my unit. Had a good look for my assailant but couldn't see her, thank fuck. Local church group choir were entertaining about fifteen patients in the dining area with carols.

Get handed the observation file to do my hour. Had to check certain people at specific intervals, assess their mental state. Three suicide risks, one intrusive behaviour due to hypomania, and the last one recently added to the list because her family couldn't make it to visit given the long drive and the weather. She was the lady in the green dress, a shade of green similar to the light flaking paint on the corridor walls. Upset. Feeling abandoned. Little to no response to interactions or reassurance.

Did laps of the unit, eyes peeled, ten-minute intervals. Playing along with the jollity and joviality with the patients on my route, festive cheer breaking up the usual routines of ward life. No incidents as I hand over the file to the next staff for their turn at the top of the hour. No respite as a congregation gathered at the far end harangue for smoke time. I take a walkie-talkie and unclip the fire door as the folks file out with their fags out ready.

Lead them down the stairs to the courtyard with the high fence, no smoking rooms inside these days. Stand at the door lighting them up one at a time. The lady in the green dress, all done up and nowhere to go, preoccupied. Spark the lighter and she inhales but doesn't go out. Instead she goes to my left. I light another one from the queue with my peripheral vision doing overtime. Split second. The hand with the cigarette drops from the mouth to the dress. Singe. Fuck. Snatch the fag and lash it on the floor. Press the ring of flaming green material with my palms and thankfully it stops the burn. A bit longer and the dress would have gone up like a fountain firework. She weeps softly as I speak into the walkie talkie and staff come running. I mime what she did and then do a talk mime and they nod and walk her back upstairs.

Christmas eve.

The smokers are having a singsong and then they say they've got a surprise for us staff. I join them with a cig, not giving a fuck if they grass me up. Couldn't care less, but they never did. "Go on, what's *this surprise then?"*

"You'll find out in a minute," one says, and they laugh together.

They throw their stumps in the ashtray and go back inside then I lock up and follow them, flicking the door shut and reactivating the alarm.

Sat on the table at the top of the ward and saw what they'd done. They must have been out earlier in the day, those that were allowed, and had sneaked in a spread for us staff from them. Out they came out of the patient's kitchen with plates of sandwiches and pasties and little cakes.

"Surprise!" One shouted. "Merry Christmas. We'll look after you lot seeing as you look after us the rest of the year," shouted another.

I could have bloody wept.

Radio on full blast. The Pogues. Fairy Tale Of New York.

No fairy tales here, in England, in the infirmary, on the unit, behind the locked doors, with the flaking paint on those walls.

Drug companies raking it in, folk like us giving what we could of the human factor, providing those intangibles that were more than just words, that seem to go missing when reducing life experience to neurotransmitters or whatever else, as best we could, on Christmas Eve.

Shift ending. Stood in the dining room near the nine-foot tree the local gardening centre donated with my coat on, waiting for the handover to finish. Laughing at a funny story a patient is telling. Tired, maybe a bit emotional for many reasons, looking back. Lost in thought.

Footsteps.

"You'll not call me a cunt again you swine." I glimpse tinsel looped over my head and down past my eyes and round my neck as I try and place the voice. Then it dawns on me, my assailant is back with a vengeance.

Dragged backwards. Struggling with my balance. I grab the tree to keep me up. The entire thing topples towards me as I fall backwards. One set of fingers under the tinsel. The other activating my alarm, setting off the electric orchestra of emergency.

Patients shouting, "Ger off 'im."

"Towd you I'd get you, you bastard," she says through a cackle.

More footsteps and another scuffle as the tinsel slackens. Me on the floor, with the Christmas tree on top of me. Baubles rolling all over.

Couldn't help but laugh.
In the infirmary, on the ward, on Christmas Eve.
Radio blaring: ...and the bells were ringing out...

Was lost in thought to crazy days in times past until I was jerked back into the present moment by the stewardess.

She said, "Landing soon, please fasten your seatbelt. You were miles away."

"I certainly was. But now I'm coming home."

"Have a wonderful Christmas."

"Thank you. You too. You're beautiful by the way. You aren't single by any chance?"

She said, "Fuck off."

So I did. In a taxi, from the airport to Atherton Town. Home.

Christmas In Blighty or Nunchucks and Mistletoe

A Christmas Drink

December twenty third. Atherton Cemetery blanketed in snow. Me, with my big coat on and a can of Carling, blinking away the falling snowflakes.

Crouching at my mate Ronnie Finkell's grave.

Staring at the headstone, thinking how weird it was his body was just under my feet. Probably warmer than me.

He once held the Northern Area Flyweight belt. The Hag Fold Hurricane. I remember his first pro-fight. Was in his corner carrying the water bottle. First round. He got rattled with a rabbit punch that stung so hard it made *me* piss blood. Ref separates them and Ronnie comes over. Goes to climb out the ring.

"What you doing?" I said.

"He got me reet in't piss pump. I'm going home. My name's Van Gogh and I'm off," he said.

I gave him an openhanded slap across the kisser. His bottom lip wobbled and he looked at me like I'd pissed on his kitten.

"It's a kidney, not a piss pump. He caught you because you were prancing about. Tuck your elbows in and get dancing."

"It hurts, you dickhead."

"Well hit him and don't get hit then. You've trained for this, now go and show what you can do. Stop crying for God's sake."

"Well, you didn't need to slap me."

"Just pretend he's nicked your bong."

"Right. I'll fucking have him."

The tears stopped in their tracks as his jaws ground the gumshield. And that was all it took. Never lost another pro fight.

I stood up and poured the rest of the beer onto the grass.

Some fella shouted, "Oy, you'd best not be having a piss."

"Don't be ridiculous. Sling it, you whopper," I said.

Looked back at the headstone. "Merry Christmas, mate."

A Christmas Blessing

Coming up to seven. Snow turning to grey slush as I trudge up Market Street. Flashes of lights shaped like stars the council had put up. Bustle of last-minute shoppers and drinkers smoking outside the pubs. Turned right by the Wheatsheaf and headed to St. Richard's church on Mayfield Street to catch the early evening mass.

I wasn't sure about God, in fact if He did exist I wouldn't mind a quiet word with Him to be honest. But there was something about the hymns and the reverence that I couldn't quite let go of at this time of year.

Hoped Father Percival Kay had mellowed. Long story short, I'd bugged the confession booth and two people subsequently died. Not my finest moment.

Walked in, most of the benches already brimming.

"You. Out," he shouted. Nope, no mellowing. Everybody turned round.

"Can't we move on?"

"Out."

What would Ronnie have said? Something popped in my head. It was his riposte when he was informed he'd been banned from JR's off-license for pinching a penny toffee. It just came out: "A penny toffee? You want to grab your piss flaps and get a grip."

"What? Just get out!"

Can't reason with some people. Slammed the door behind me as I left.

Muttered, "Nobhead," and slinked off to my apartment, one of the new ones across from the Punchbowl pub. Got a beer from the fridge and flicked on the telly. Some service, a choir singing.

Drank myself to sleep, passing out on the sofa after watching a *Gremlins* DVD, trying to remind myself of the Christmas magic from childhood that was melting quicker than the snow.

Stocking Fillers

9am. Christmas Eve. Atherton Town. Rough as a hedgehog's ballsack.

Woken by the zap of the doorbell.

I click unlock and hear footsteps up the stairs, eye up to the peephole, baseball bat by my side.

A woman, white bob hat with a red bobble, blonde curls framing her face. Open up as far as the chain lets me.

"Are you Mr. Gibfield?"

"You the police?"

"No, why what've you done."

"Nothing, but it's only them what call me Mr. Gibfield, usually while being arrested."

"I don't want to arrest you. I want to hire you."

"You're dafter than you look."

"I was told you were a P.I."

"Some people would claim those letters stand for pissing idiot."

She burst out laughing. Just before the tears.

Her Story came flooding out. Boyfriend being a nasty bastard so she dumps him. He's not happy and now he's blackmailing her, threatening to release intimate images taken at happier times. Revenge porn.

I use my one and only real skill I'd honed over the years: Listening.

She finishes her tale and wipes her face with a sheet of kitchen roll.

"What does he do?"

"He's a proctologist."

"Dr Arsehole, eh?"

That triggers a giggle. She says, "You think you can help me?"

"Can't promise anything. I'll see what I can do."

She reaches into her purse and pulls out a wedge of money.

I wave it away.

"Sort me out later, if my plan works."

"What are you going to do?"

"The less you know, the better."

She insists with the cash but I decline. I still had a few grand left over from backing Ronnie to win the belt, otherwise I'd have snatched her hand off, truth be told. Or maybe not. Tis the season for good deeds and all that jazz.

She wrote down her name, April, telephone number and address, alongside Dr Arsehole's location.

"I'll be in touch."

She nods and leaves.

Her perfume lingers with her sense of reassurance. Me, taking a deep breath and running through a scenario in my head, hoping I don't fuck things up. Tried to shower the headache away.

Put my big coat on, rummaged through the kitchen drawer for some plastic bags and headed out. Kicked up grey slush, melting snow mixed with oil from the road.

Walked to Max Spielmann and on the way back nipped into the butcher's next to the Punchbowl. I told him what I wanted and he gave me a funny look.

He said, "People usually have turkeys or geese." Grinned.

"Really, I hadn't noticed."

"No need to be sarcastic, it's just unusual."

"These are strange days," I said and fixed him with my best stare.

He must have thought I was fucked out of my head on drugs. It sped up the transaction and clipped the banter.

Market Street, heavy foot traffic, frying fish and bakeries wafting in the cold air. My mouth was drooling but my stomach wouldn't process anything substantial so settled for a corned beef and onion roll from Bar Be Chic and went home.

I needed assistance and made a phone call to Simon Braggins, former doorman turned gigolo:

"Hairband, merry Christmas. I need a hand."

"If you keep calling me hairband you'll be shit out of luck."

"You can't be so sensitive. People go bald."

"Are you winding me up?"

"Sorry. No, I'm serious." I told him the tale.

"No bother. What tools do you think I should bring?"

"I'll leave that up to you. Pick Lieutenant Ferry up on your way."

"Do we really need Fez? You know he causes carnage."

"You never know when carnage can be useful."

They arrived in under half an hour.

"Merry Christmas, lads. Check out your Christmas stockings," I said, pointing to the bags.

Fez seemed to really think I'd got him a present. Opened his bag, recoiled his head back and shouted, "Whoa, what the fuck is this, you dickhead." Si peeked a look and laughed.

I explained the plan of action and they nodded along.

Fez said, "Soon as it's dark. In the meantime I think we should visit Mark."

"Fair shout."

Jumped in Si's car and shot off.

The Visit Of The Three Wise Men

DS Mark Reed had been suspended without pay from the police force after getting coked out of his eyeballs and causing a near riot in The Mill bar with a poem. I wasn't sure if he still held us responsible for his descent into drugs, although his dabble as a bard was entirely his own doing. He'd been checked into the psychiatric unit.

On the drive to the infirmary I said to Si, "You've lost weight. Everything ok?"

"Gigolo overtime. Raking it in. Plenty of lonely ladies this time of year. Feel like I've been milked dry. Got balls like raisins."

Fez just shook his head.

We buzzed the ward doorbell and the staff let us in. Went to fetch Mark.

He was at the top of the corridor in a side room. Came out, had a look, recognised us and said, "Well, well, well. If it isn't the three wise men." He had a blanket over his shoulders and straight away I wondered which one of us would say it. I was very tempted myself.

"Alright, mate," Fez said, "Just thought we'd see how you were doing, cheer you up, like."

Si said, "You could do with a haircut and a shave. Do you want me to get the clippers off the staff?"

Mark padded down to us with a right look on his face. Said, "How I'm doing? Cheer me up? My career's in tatters and this prat is banging on about my hair?"

"Just trying to help, mate," Si said.

A crowd of staff and patients had gathered.

"It'll be a cold day in Hell when I need help from a prostitute, an idiot who thinks he's a P.I. because he's read the fucking novels – "

Si looked around at half the ward who'd burst out laughing and said loudly, "I think you'll find I'm a gigolo actually, Mark."

Fez creased up.

Mark turned to Fez and said, "I don't know what you're laughing at. You're one loose screw away from going feral up rucks like the British version of Rambo First Blood. The three wise men? More like the three absolute dickheads." He swished his blanket and added, "Staff, show these people to the door."

Si was still embarrassed and I just knew he'd say it. He shouted, "At least try and enjoy your Christmas dinner. If you can't be bothered with the turkey there's always pigs in blankets."

"Staff, get them three out before I go ballistic," Mark shouted.

We crossed the car park to Si's car and Fez said, "That actually went better than I expected."

Bearing Gifts or The Northern Shinobi

We still had a bit of time before dark, so went back to mine and played poker swigging cold beers.

"What tools did you pick?" I asked Si.

"Went for the nunchucks in the end."

Fez threw his cards down, stood up and stretched, flicked open the curtain and said, "Right lads, let's get the party started."

Drove through town, rehearsing what we were going to do, and parked on the carpark of the Talbot pub on Wigan Road. Dr Arsehole's place was a house on the new estate. Scoped it out.

Fez said, "Right, you two figure out if you can get in on ground level. I'll check the skylight on the roof. If you can manage it, I'll stay up there as lookout."

I said, "What is it with you, roofs and skylights?"

"Have you been trained in reconnaissance?"

"No."

"Well shut up then."

With that, he scaled the roof.

Si said, "I can see him through the curtains in the living room. He's on his own." He crouched down and scuttled under the window ledge to the front door. Put his hand in the letterbox.

"What you doing?" I whispered

"There might be a key on a piece of string."

"Do people still do that these days?"

"Soon find out. Oh, shit."

"What?"

"My hand's stuck."

"Are you having me on?"

"No, I'm being serious, it's pissing stuck."

I just couldn't believe this. Gripped his arm at the wrist and yanked it back. The letterbox clattered like a starting pistol. I grabbed Si's collar and we rolled behind the bushes.

Our revenge porn merchant opened the door, looked both ways and muttered something before slamming it and locking up.

"We could have just tried the handle and walked in. Back door might be open," Si said.

It was. I texted Fez: *We're in*. Got a thumbs-up in return. Slowly depressed the door handle and crept through the kitchen.

"Are you ready," I said to Si.

"Born ready and bold as brass," he grinned.

I lead the way. Opened the adjoining door and strolled in. Did a double-take.

Our target was sat on the couch. Fez was sat behind him, gripping him in a sleeper hold with a hand over his mouth. He shrugged and said, "Nipped in while you two were fannying about. Was going to come down the chimney seeing as it's Christmas but it's a gas fire." I wasn't sure if he was joking. "I'll leave yous to it and get back up on roof as lookout."

Si pushed his top lip up exposing his teeth and said in a Bugs Bunny voice, "What's up, Doc?"

The Doc just sat there, gobsmacked.

"I've always wanted to do that," Si said.

Doc found his voice. "What the hell do you think you're playing at? Get the fuck out of my property you troglodytes."

"Is this where I nunchuck him?"

"Nunchuck me? How dare you." He reached for the phone but I yanked the wire out.

I said, "Tell me about revenge porn, Doctor Arsehole. If we can be reasonable we won't need nunchucks."

Blood drained from his face. "None of your fucking

business."

"It is actually. You shan't fuck with my clients."

"Clients? Just who do you think you are you fucking scumbags."

"Si, I think it's nunchuck time."

Out cold.

Pig's head out of one bag and a Polaroid camera out of the other.

Plenty of cheeky snaps.

Wrote on the back of one:

Leave her alone or else.
Two can play at this game.
Merry Christmas Doctor Arsehole.
From Nun Chuck.

Searched and found the digital camera. Bagged it and the laptop just in case.

We were heading for the back door, a job well done, when we heard commotion coming from outside.

Si chanced a glance through the front window and saw a small crowd had gathered. I went over and heard, "Look, Father Christmas has let himself go. Talk about bad Santa," and a rupture of laughter. Dawned on me that Fez had been spotted on the roof. Odds on someone had phoned the police.

I said to Si, "I fucking told him about knocking about on roofs."

"Shit. What are we going to do?"

"Fucked if I know, half the street are out."

I saw it through the window before I heard it. Some kind of flash grenades were going off and pumping out billows of red smoke. We dashed through the door and out onto the street and pushed through the crowd disoriented by the plumes. Spotted Fez already nearing Si's car with his jet black fleece turned inside out now yellow and we ran after him.

"I worry about you sometimes," I said to Fez as we climbed in.

He gave me his trademark wild shark's grin and winked as Si put his foot down.

Mistletoe and Wine. And A Good Few Pints Of Lager. Plus a violin.

7pm Christmas Eve. Showered, shaved and dressed. Thought I'd make an effort instead of looking like I'd been dragged through a hedge. White oxford shirt underneath a navy suit with a woollen overcoat. Topped off with my black Kangol 507 flat cap.

Light snow falling. Crowds on the streets outside the pubs. Ale and fag smoke. Aftershave and perfume. Raucous laughter and clicking heels.

Pushed past the crowds to my van on the car park near the sunbed shop whose window emanated blue light.

Drove down Leigh Road to Howe Bridge. April's place. An apartment across from St Michael's.

She opened the door wearing a little red dress that took the wind out of me. Smiled beneath cobalt eyes.

"You've dressed up for me."

"The outfit's for going out in, actually, Mr Gibfield."

"Jacob."

Stepped back and led me inside.

Low light. Candles flickered. Eartha Kitt's *Santa Baby* from the music player. I had no illusions she was out of my league, we were talking at least four divisions. Spiked any romantic thoughts.

Handed over the bag with the gear. "You can either

boot them up, wipe them and send them back with a Dear John letter telling Dr Arsehole to permanently leave you alone. Or you can smash them up with a hammer and lash the remnants up the rucks. Entirely up to you."

"How sure are you it's over?" She said.

Flashed her a couple of Polaroids. "Pretty sure."

Laughter.

"How much do I owe you?"

Shook my head. "Consider it a Christmas miracle brought to you by the three wise men of Atherton Town. Have a merry Christmas."

Turned to go and she put her hand on my arm. "One second," she said. Came back from the mantlepiece with a piece of mistletoe. Held it above her head.

Hands round her waist. I didn't need asking twice.

She slid her mouth from mine, whispered into my ear, "I don't go out for another half an hour." Pushed my hands down to her arse and hitched up her dress as she licked my neck.

Heavy smell of spirits and wine. Looked over her shoulder, saw nine-tenths of a bottle of Merlot empty.

I couldn't gauge whether the moment was the relief, the drink, the season or whether it was genuine attraction. An element of self-loathing ruled out the latter and I didn't want to feel like I'd taken advantage. So, very reluctantly, I pulled away slowly, smiled, and said the dickhead thing, "It's not you. Trust me, it's definitely not you. It's me." Like I say, the dickhead thing, but at least it was the truth. Also, the last client I'd gone to bed with wound up dead. Not a fate to tempt.

I could have said, "If you weren't pissed out of your face it might be different," but I didn't fancy a hard slap across the chops.

She took a deep breath and shrugged. "Suit

yourself."

Let myself out. As I was coming down the stairs, I shouted, "Have a good one."

"You too, Mr P.I. I agree, it must stand for pissing idiot."

Indeed. Walked into the cold, unforgiving winter air, thinking at least she knew where I lived if she wanted me sober. Wouldn't be holding my breath, that's for sure. I was trying to pinpoint the exact time when life suddenly exploded into complexities as I made my way to meet the lads. Dumped the van, slinked through the drinkers on the street and gave up pondering as I entered The Mill bar.

Lieutenant Ferry and Si were in the corner with pints and shots. Sat down in the chair they'd guarded for me.

Fez said, "You've took your time, what've you been doing? Is that lipstick on your neck? You've not been shagging your clients again, have you? Where's your service ethics?"

"Nowt happened. Nevermind that, I need a pint. So does he," I said, pointing to Si, "you look dehydrated to fuck."

"Milked dry, man. Bollocks like bloody raisins."

It just clicked to me, "Lads, we've forgot Colin."

PC Colin Chase was another old mate of ours, joined the cops with Mark. Unlike Mark he hadn't been suspended without pay, but he had been told in no uncertain terms to check himself into a drug and alcohol rehab. Whether it was the pressure of the job or the simple fact he just liked cocaine and ale and found them increasingly moreish was debatable and up to the rehab people to help him work out.

Wasn't allowed visitors because he'd been caught trying to bribe people to bring stuff in for him. So Fez got his phone out and facetimed him.

Colin's face popped up and filled the screen. He said,

"Alright, folks. Where are you? In a pub? I bet you're in a pub."

"Drinking responsibly," Fez said. Si and I burst out laughing.

"Shut up you dickhead," Colin said.

Si got his debit card out and poured some salt from a shaker onto the tabletop. Started chopping it up and separating it into lines. Nudged Fez who swung the camera down to show Colin.

Colin's beady eyes came right up to the lens and he said, "You rotten bastards. You're going to have to send me some, I'm crawling up the walls. I've been thinking about it. A lot.

Right, what you need to do is get a bottle of aftershave, empty it, wash it out, fill it with whisky. Or, get a tube of Pringles, slide half of the crisps out, tape a baggie – just a small eye opener so it doesn't look suss – onto the back of one of the crisps in the middle and put the rest back on top. Then, you've got to glue the foil back down so if the staff test it they can't tell it's been tampered with.

Or you could buy a drone and fly it to my bedroom window with a magnet stuck to the bottom. Put a piece of lead in the bag of coke so it sticks to the drone and camouflage it so no one can see it on the underside.

Or you could send me a box of washing powder and put some of the good stuff in. You'd have to mark the crystals with permanent marker so I could differentiate which powder was which. Painstaking, I agree, but undetectable to the untrained eye. Essentially foolproof.

What do you reckon?"

Fez said, "I reckon you need to get a fucking grip and accept the help you're being offered."

"So you're not going to send me anything?"

"Yes, we're sending you thoughts and prayers on

your journey to recovery. We're rooting for you."

Colin just shook his head and started ranting and raving so Fez ended the call.

Pub crawl. Wheatsheaf, Jolly Nailor, Pendle Witch, Red Lion, Weaver's Rest till closing. Traditional British boozers. Can't beat them.

One place left open. Mountain Dew.

"Dew till two?"

"What do you think?"

We walked in. Four deep rammed at the bar. Raucous. Everyone dolled up and a jovial atmosphere. Speakers blaring.

Some geezer I'd known for decades comes over and I recognise him immediately but for the life of me can't place his name.

He says, "I'm up next. Singing Gangster's Parasite. Coolio." Points at the karaoke.

"Paradise."

"It is innit. Nowhere else in the world like the Dew on Christmas Eve."

I suspected he was right, for all sorts of reasons. "I meant the title."

"What's vital?"

"Nevermind. Have a good one."

"You too."

He gets up on the stage and serenades the place.

I'm dragged through the bar by my wrist. April. She takes me into a cubicle and gives me a blowjob. Romance alive and well. I'm more pissed than she is at this point. I finish. She looks up and says, "Merry Christmas. Call me."

I try and say, "I will do," but I can't get my words out proper, slurring.

Last-orders bell rings and not long after we all pile out onto Market Street. I look for her but she's nowhere to be seen. Si and Fez pop their heads out of the kebab shop doorway. "Where've you been?"

I try and tap my nose but I keep missing.

"Fucking lightweight," Si laughs.

Hanging about for food, the cold night air sobering me up. Light snow falling. They come out with three big pizza boxes and Fez says, "Follow me."

Leads us round the back of St John the Baptists Church, where the old market used to bustle.

Gone now. Like the job centre.

Scaffolding. Leads the way. Si looks at me as if to say, "Where's he going?" I shake my head and we start climbing, following his lead.

We end up on top of the church. "Just what is it with you and roofs?" I say to Fez, who doesn't respond. Instead he leans over and pulls across a black box. Out comes his violin. Si shakes his head. Says, "Just when you think you've seen it all."

"I really, really worry about him sometimes."

Fez ignores us and tucks the violin under his chin. Gets straight into it. I think he's going for The Pogues: Fairytale of New York. That song again. Wouldn't be Christmas without it.

A fair crowd down around the Obelisk get it and start singing along, looking around for the source of the music but can't see us.

Our fiddler switches gears and fires into the hymn Jerusalem. Find myself singing along to Blake's words.

Bangs puncture the night. Mostly fireworks, probably one dodgy Ford Escort backfiring and maybe even the odd gunshot as the town sees in Christmas Day.

I saw the rows of red brick terraces, the fields, and in the distance Winter Hill at Rivington Pike.

It might not be the best place in the world. But all

through Christmas the locals clothed the homeless and made sure the less fortunate got a Christmas box. A fifteen-foot tree glowing with lights shone up at us. Glasses smashing, folks scrapping. I thought I could make out a couple shagging down the side of Weaver's Rest.

It was our home town whether we liked it or not.

I didn't buy the deterministic idea that the future was mapped out for you. It was necessary to reach out and make of it what you could.

I said to Si, "Can't wait to see the back of two thousand and nineteen."

He said, "Twenty twenty will be our year. Things can't get any worse can they?"

I said, "You honestly reckon Two thousand and twenty will be a good year or are you just saying it to make me feel better?"

He said, "I'm a very deep thinker. I'm telling you, twenty twenty is going to be good. Definitely."

"Categorically," said the Lieutenant.

They seemed sure so I went with them, nodding along, letting them convince me and convincing myself. "I agree. A hundred percent."

How wrong can you get? The three wise men of Atherton, eh? Mark was right all along. The three absolute dickheads, more like.

Author's Notes

A version of the story Jacob tells in Red Devil's Flat about Benny Big Bollock being injected was previously published as *It's Over Now in Saturday's Asylum* by Shotgun Honey and is in the short story collection *Noir Medley*.

The epilogue is made up of versions of two stories. The first of which, *and the bells were ringing out*, was published by Paul D. Brazill at *Punknoir magazine*. The second was published as *Nunchucks and Mistletoe* by Craig Douglas at *Close To The Bone*.

I was born in Bolton General in the April of 1982 and brought back to Atherton Town a couple of days later where I grew up. I've also lived in Hag Fold, Howe Bridge and Leigh. As a proud Atherton resident I figured that rather than make up a fictional place for the story, why not use my home town for the setting?

I did obviously use real locations, however I wish to clearly state that the story is entirely and completely fictional and in no way a reflection of the actual places or the fine folks of said places.

I used the streets named in the book purely for narrative and plot purposes (and to illustrate our location in the middle of Leigh, Wigan, Bolton and Manchester) and I reiterate categorically that all the happenings in this book are completely made up by me.

While I'm here I also want to thank Saint Richard's primary school on Flapper Fold Lane and the teachers there from 1987 to when I left in 1993 who helped nurture my love of reading and writing from a very early age, as did my English teachers at St Mary's.

I want to say thanks to all my family on both sides and my friends from Atherton Town who I've known throughout my life. There are way too many to list and I won't even try because I don't want to forget a name, but you all know who you are. Cheers folks.

If you the reader have got this far, I want to thank you sincerely for the support in buying the book.

Thank you.

About the Author

L.A. Sykes was born in Bolton General Hospital and grew up in Atherton in Greater Manchester, England.

He went to St Richard's Primary School Atherton, St Mary's High School Astley and afterwards attended their Sixth Form College.

He studied psychology and criminology at University of Central Lancashire, leaving university to work for the NHS in acute psychiatric inpatient units.

He spent two years working with people with disabilities with Wigan Council.

He is the author of *Noir Medley*: collected short fiction volume one, featuring most of his published short stories, flash fiction and podcast work, and the novella The Hard Cold Shoulder.

He is a fan of Leigh rugby league. After gaining promotion to Super League in 2022 they entered a new era, successfully rebranding from Centurions to Leigh Leopards. They lifted the 2023 Challenge Cup for the third time in their history and achieved their best top-flight campaign in almost half a century. His dad Stephen's father, Harry Sykes, played for the club in the 1930s.

Whilst working with people with disabilities he met and shook hands with Queen Elizabeth II when Her Majesty came to visit Leigh Sports Village where his team were based. Although this is something he very, very rarely mentions…

Printed in Great Britain
by Amazon